Now... a
Harlequin
romance
by Anne Mather
comes to life
on the movie screen

starring
KEIR DULLEA · SUSAN PENHALIGON

Leopard in the Snow

Guest Stars
KENNETH MORE · BILLIE WHITELAW

featuring GORDON THOMSON as MICHAEL
and JEREMY KEMP as BOLT

Produced by JOHN QUESTED and CHRIS HARROP
Screenplay by ANNE MATHER and JILL HYEM
Directed by GERRY O'HARA

An Anglo-Canadian Co-Production

OTHER
Harlequin Romances
by REBECCA STRATTON

1748—THE GOLDEN MADONNA
1770—FAIRWINDS
1799—THE BRIDE OF ROMANO
1816—CASTLES IN SPAIN
1839—RUN FROM THE WIND
1858—ISLAND OF DARKNESS
1883—AUTUMN CONCERTO
1898—FIREBIRD
1913—THE FLIGHT OF THE HAWK
1942—THE FIRE AND THE FURY
1955—MOON TIDE
1976—THE GODDESS OF MAVISU
1991—ISLE OF THE GOLDEN DRUM
2006—PROUD STRANGER
2018—CHATEAU D'ARMOR
2036—THE ROAD TO GAFSA
2050—GEMINI CHILD
2078—GIRL IN A WHITE HAT
2091—INHERIT THE SUN
2106—MORE THAN A DREAM

Many of these titles are available at your local bookseller
or through the Harlequin Reader Service.

For a free catalogue listing all available Harlequin Romances,
send your name and address to:

HARLEQUIN READER SERVICE,
M.P.O. Box 707, Niagara Falls, N.Y. 14302
Canadian address: Stratford, Ontario, Canada N5A 6W4

or use order coupon at back of books.

The Sign of the Ram

by

REBECCA STRATTON

Harlequin Books

TORONTO • LONDON • NEW YORK • AMSTERDAM • SYDNEY

Original hardcover edition published in 1977
by Mills & Boon Limited

ISBN 0-373-02131-3

Harlequin edition published January 1978

PRINTED IN U.S.A.

CHAPTER ONE

SARA was uncertain at the moment whether it was anger or embarrassment that was primarily responsible for the colour in her cheeks and the bright gleam in her grey eyes, but both emotions tangled in her chaotic mind and anger seemed to have the upper hand at present.

She was no novice on the subject of antiques, for her grounding had been long and thorough. Ever since she was old enough to be trusted to move about among the treasures of her father's London gallery she had lived with the knowledge of beautiful things from the past. She had known little else but the business of antiques since her earliest days and until now she had felt confident enough, even in a foreign city and with virtually no knowledge of the language, to cope with anything that came along.

It was partly resentment for the first niggle of doubt about her own competence that caused her anger, and quite naturally extended to include the man who aroused it. She had been certain she could cope with the running of her uncle's antique business while he was away on an extended honeymoon with his new Italian wife, and so far she had done so easily.

He had assured her that the majority of his clientele were English and American tourists, so that language was not likely to present any difficulties, and his prophecy had proved correct for the most part. She found Venice every bit as delightful as its reputation and, even though she had so far spent only four days there, she was already enchanted by it and quite happy to stay the couple of months expected of her. The city and its people were charming, and the man who now faced her was the first and only incident to make her doubt both the wisdom of her offer to her uncle and her own abilities.

He was probably about six feet tall, which gave him a distinct advantage over her own slight build, and he was fiercely and aggressively masculine, with dark eyes that regarded her with a brooding look of suspicion and impatience. There were traces of silver grey in the thick dark hair above his ears, although it was doubtful if he had yet reached forty, and the set of his features was in keeping with the apparent character of the man—arrogant and suggestive of ruthlessness.

A jug stood on the glass counter between them, its simple lines and dragon decoration making it appear far too commonplace a thing to be the cause of such angry discussion. Sara had bought it in good faith the day before from a young Italian, and paid him what she knew to be a fair price for a reproduction, even though the reproduction itself was quite valuable as an antique.

What she resented most of all was the suggestion that she had paid over far less than it was worth; that seemed to be important to him even though he claimed she had no right to it at all, for she had never before been accused of being unscrupulous. Resting one hand on the cool glazed earthenware where the handle joined the swell of the base was an unconscious reminder to the man facing her that possession was nine points of the law, and she glared a challenge at her accuser that dared him to deny her that right.

'I bought the jug in good faith, *signore*, and the price was fair!'

6

It was annoying to feel so unsure of herself when she knew she was perfectly correct, no matter what that ominous dark face the other side of the counter suggested. The man glanced at the sign that hung outside the shop before turning back to her once more. A board suspended from chains in the manner of an inn sign showed a gilded representation of a ram with above it the words, *Il Ariete d'Oro*, and below it in one corner, *Prop. R. Ramson*.

'You are Signorina Ramson?'

'Yes, I am, but——'

'It would appear, Signorina Ramson, that you are either less than honest or else you know less about your business than you should. Not only did you purchase an article for much less than it is worth, but you made no inquiry as to whether or not you were entitled to buy it at all!'

'Oh, now just a moment!' The colour burned bright in Sara's cheeks and there was no doubt at all now that it was anger that caused it. 'I can't be expected to cross-examine everyone who comes in here with something to sell, it simply isn't reasonable! I'm neither dishonest nor a fool, or my uncle would never have entrusted me to run his business for him while he's away, and since you have implied both, I insist you apologise right now!'

Her slim figure, completely disguised by a loose cotton smock, was drawn up straight as she glared across the counter at him, and there was little sign of the nervousness that lurked only just below the anger in her eyes. Honey-fair hair drawn back from her face gave a somewhat severe look to her small oval face, but her twenty-four years sat lightly on her, and it was doubtful if the man who faced her thought her any more than twenty

7

or twenty-one. It was a mistake that many people made.

He would not apologise, she realised it even before she had finished demanding that he should, but he raised a brow that suggested her response surprised him. 'I will apologise willingly when I see cause to, *signorina*, but at the moment I am forced to see you as either dishonest or inexperienced—I hope it is the latter. If it proves to be so then I will return to you the price that you paid for the jug and say no more about it.'

'But I can't do that!' It was not easy to be adamant with that relentless gaze upon her, but she could not simply part with the jug again at cost price, to someone she had never seen before. Her uncle trusted her to act in the best interests of his business, and such a transaction would be very bad business indeed. 'You must see that I can't sell an article for the same price as I paid for it when all I have is your word that it belongs to you!'

Dark eyes narrowed and glittered in the shadowy light of the shop. 'And you doubt my word, *signorina*?'

'Can you blame me?' She sounded defensive, and resented that too, for she refused to see herself in the wrong. 'You must see that I can't just blindly trust everyone who comes in here—if I did that I *would* be a fool! Are you telling me that the man who brought it in was a thief? That he stole it from you? If that's so then I'd better call the police and let them sort it out.'

'There is no need for such measures, *signorina*, it is a matter only for common sense! The article is mine and I wish it to be returned to me with a minimum of fuss, that is all. You cannot be the loser.'

Sara was no longer sure what she believed. His argument sounded disturbingly convincing, but yet he had offered no explanation as to how the jug came to be offered for sale without his knowledge or consent. She had to admit, however grudgingly, that she was already half convinced, but it was too flimsy a foundation on which to base a decision to hand over the jug for no more than she had paid for it, and she shook her head firmly.

'I'm sorry, *signore*, I can't do it.'

She felt a small sinking sensation in the pit of her stomach when he regarded her for a second longer in silence, eyes narrowed and straight mouth set hard in a tight line. 'I will not pay you a profit to return my family's possessions when you have no right to them in the first place, *signorina*! But perhaps you will be more readily convinced by a legal advocate!'

Sara, swallowed hard, a thudding beat in her heart when she visualised herself becoming involved in a legal battle for the return of the jug. It was an awkward situation, and she must avoid a legal involvement at all costs; her uncle would be horrified at the very idea. If ever a situation called for compromise this was it, and she flicked an anxious tongue over her lips as she attempted one.

'If you're right about it being yours——'

'Be assured I am, *signorina*!'

'I—I'd be willing to return it to the same man who sold it to me. It shouldn't be difficult for you to produce him,' she added swiftly when she saw the way he frowned. 'I assume you know who it is since you were so unwilling to have the police brought in.'

'You will not accept my word?'

'I can't!' Sara carefully avoided looking at him. 'You must realise that; the jug is valuable, even as a reproduction.'

9

'A reproduction?' Sara almost panicked. She knew it was a reproduction, and yet by expressing disbelief this man made her almost doubt her own conviction. 'You are mistaken, *signorina*. I suggest you study your subject more thoroughly!'

She had taken just about as much as she intended taking from this autocratic stranger, and she laid both hands on the earthenware jug, her eyes bright and angry. 'I have been thoroughly taught by my father, *signore*, and I've been working among antiques ever since I was a schoolgirl. I know my subject very well, and I challenge you to prove me wrong!'

Briefly the dark eyes narrowed as they searched her flushed face keenly. 'You sound very confident, *signorina*.'

'I am!' The merest flicker of doubt in his voice gave her the courage to go on. 'You believe this to be Urbino Maiolica, don't you?'

Why on earth she should feel so strangely reluctant to disillusion him, she had no idea, and plainly he did not mean to accept her opinion. It showed in the eyes that searched rapidly over her face for some sign that she was attempting to trick him.

'We have never had reason to doubt its authenticity, *signorina*. Do you now tell me that we have been deceived all these years?'

'I'm afraid so, if you believe it's genuine Urbino.' Her reluctance to tell him the truth was there in her voice, and the man looked at her for a second and frowned. Her sympathy was obviously something he did not expect. 'It was produced by a factory in Bologna some time in the middle of the last century. They specialised in making copies of Urbino and Luca della Robbia. It's very good, *signore*, but it isn't genuine Urbino.'

'I cannot speak with enough expertise to argue with you, *signorina*, but it is possible to consult someone better qualified, then we shall see.' He reached over and Sara hastily relinquished her hold on the jug rather than find her hand enclosed by his long brown fingers. 'Whatever the truth of its identity, the jug belongs to my family and I insist upon its return.'

Sara's heart lurched sickeningly as she visualised him taking it with or without her consent, and she did not see what on earth she could do to stop him if he took it by force. Once more she ventured to suggest a compromise, seeing it as the best way out of a difficult situation.

'I'm willing to return it to the young man who brought it to me, I can promise you that. I can't do any more.'

He considered for a second, then jerked his head in a brief nod as he turned away. 'You may expect to see my son again within the hour, *signorina*; we will have this matter settled! *Arrivederci!*'

His abrupt departure took her by surprise, and for a second Sara watched in silence as long legs carried him to the door in lengthy, impatient strides that suggested he was still angry at her refusal to recognise his claim. Recovering herself hastily when he was on the point of opening the door into the street, she called after him.

'*Buon giorno, signore!*'

It wasn't until he went past the window that she realised she had no idea at all who he was, and picking up the jug again, she gazed at it thoughtfully for a moment or two. Whoever he was he laid great store by the jug. Either that or he was a man who did not easily relinquish what he held, which seemed a likely explanation on second thoughts.

It looked such a simple thing to have brought two complete strangers to the point of quarrelling, and she wondered if the man who had brought it to her would as willingly come back to reclaim it. She could recall him quite well, she was rather surprised to realise, but then he had been very charming and courteous, quite unlike the man who had just left and who claimed to be his father.

In fact it wasn't easy to accept them as father and son, for her last caller had struck her as no more than thirty-seven or eight, scarcely old enough to be father to the young gallant who had sold her the controversial jug. When she thought about it, she hoped he *would* come and reclaim it, for in retrospect the situation was quite intriguing.

Venetian glass gleamed at her from across the shop, and Sara smiled. The sun coming in through the wide, low window caught it at certain times of the day and seemingly brought it to life. It had a warm glow at its heart that seemed to pulse like a living thing, and she never tired of looking at it; it was the one thing that she actually coveted with an avidity that surprised her when she recognised it.

A trumpet-shaped bowl surmounted a stem so intricately worked and so seemingly fragile that it seemed impossible it could have been created solely by the breath of a man, no matter how skilled he might be. She felt a strange sense of excitement whenever she looked at it, dazzled and enchanted by its beauty.

Startled out of her daydream suddenly, she looked up,

and caught her breath when she recognised the man whose entrance started the bells ringing on the door and snatched her back to reality. Within the hour, the claimant of the copy Urbino had promised, and it was scarcely more than half an hour since he went striding out of the shop.

'*Signorina!*'

She would have recognised him even without the incident of the jug to remind her, for he was the kind of man who makes it hard to forget him, but he was younger than she had first thought, possibly no more than nineteen or twenty. It was having such an air of urbane charm and self-assurance that gave the impression that he was older in the first instance.

He was fractionally shorter than the man who claimed to be his father too, she recognised, and much better looking; certainly he would be less ruthless. In fact he was less sure of himself than his manner implied if she looked more closely at him, though he did an excellent job of concealing it.

He was dark in a way that she had already decided was typically Italian, except for a pair of hazel eyes between thick black lashes that looked at her for a moment in both speculation and doubt even though he smiled. He wore a light suit and a blue silk shirt, both so obviously expensive that she could not easily accept the fact that he had needed to sell the jug because he was in need of money.

'What can I say to you? I must apologise for causing you such embarrassment, of course, but I did not anticipate such a thing happening.' He spread his hands wide and shrugged broad shoulders beneath a smoothly tailored jacket. 'I am so sorry, *signorina!*'

Sara was not sure what attitude she had intended to take with him, but it was difficult not to respond to the appeal in his eyes no matter how much annoyance he had caused her. 'I accept your apology, *signore*, though I'm still at a complete loss to understand any of this.'

He put both hands on the edge of the counter, his palms flat on the warm glass, long fingers outlined by the light in the display case beneath, and leaning slightly towards her in a curiously intimate posture. 'I hope that you were not too offended by my father's manner, *signorina*. He is not a man who cares to charm the ladies, and he is angry.'

Unwilling to commit herself to either side at the moment, Sara was forced to admit that in view of events the older man probably had grounds for his anger, though it did not excuse his rudeness to her. 'Maybe he had cause to be angry, I don't know, but I do take exception to being called not only dishonest but inexperienced and incompetent too.'

'*Madre de Dio!* He said this to you?'

'More than once!'

The hazel eyes rolled heavenwards in dismay, then looked at her once more, anxiously. 'Please forgive me, *signorina*. Not for anything would I have made you the butt of my father's anger, and once more I say I am sorry. Will you forgive me?'

It was the look in his eyes that made her realise, once more, how young he was. Heaven knew why he had taken the jug and sold it, for nothing about him pointed to the likelihood of his being kept short of money, but there was something about him that was irresistibly appealing.

Her own childhood had been spent mostly in the company of adults; she had no brothers or sisters, and only two cousins of whom she saw little. Her life had been comfortable enough but filled with the talk of business and antiques, or chess which her father played enthusiastically but badly. She had spent little time with people of her own age, so that she felt less at ease with them than with someone older.

Looking at the good-looking young face the other side of the counter, she sought some reason for his acting as he had. 'Presumably you acted as you did with good reason,' she said. 'And I did promise to let you have the jug for the price I paid you for it.'

'I thought my reasons excellent, *signorina*, though my father does not have the same opinion, but I was wrong to get you involved. My father is not an easy man to defy, and you presumably would not give him back the jug.'

He was a very difficult man to defy, Sara thought ruefully, and when she thought about it, she shrank from the memory of how she had insisted he could not have the jug back at the price she had paid for it. He must have thought her very shrewd and businesslike, but whatever his opinion, he had eventually yielded to her compromise.

'I was angry enough to defy anyone,' she confessed with a trace of a smile warming her grey eyes, and he beamed in response.

It was all the encouragement he needed, she realised; he was a born charmer. 'You also, *signorina*! I too was angry and defiant. I wanted money which Carlo refused to let me have, and so I took the jug to defy him. It was an impulse.'

Presumably Carlo was his father, her erstwhile caller,

and she could well imagine him being a stern parent. 'It was a dangerous impulse,' she informed him. 'I was on the point of sending for the police when I learned that the jug had been taken without the consent of its owner!'

He shivered in mock horror, and the hazel eyes rolled heavenwards once more. 'You will forgive me, Signorina Ramson?' He smiled at her glance of surprise and shook his head. 'I learned your name from my father—it is to my regret that I did not discover it myself.'

'Your father assumed the shop was mine, that's how he found out my name. In fact it belongs to my uncle.'

He turned his head, much as the older man had, and glanced at the sign with its shiny gold interpretation of their family name, then held her gaze steadily when he turned back—more confident now that he was sure of his ground.

'The Golden Ram,' he translated. 'So R. Ramson is your uncle, eh?' His eyes flicked briefly in the direction of the room behind her, its entrance concealed by a curtain. 'Is he also here, *signorina*, or are you in complete charge of the business?'

'For the moment.' His intent was so obvious that Sara refrained from specifying just how long the moment was. 'My uncle is on honeymoon in Rimini.'

'Ah!' He extended a hand and smiled. 'I am Giovanni Cantorini, *signorina*.' Her fingers were seized and raised to his lips all in one swift and unexpected move. 'To my friends I am Gianni.' Another light touch with his lips. 'I hope that you will call me Gianni, Signorina Ramson.'

The implication was obvious; having invited her to use his intimate name, he expected her to return the compliment, and she obliged to the extent of telling him her first name. 'I'm Sara Ramson, Signor Cantorini.'

He retained his hold on her hand, his eyes bright and bold now that he was confident of not being rejected. 'You are an unexpected treasure to find in the gloom of an antique shop,' he declared. 'You surely do not stay here from choice, *signorina*.'

'Oh, but I do, I love working here!'

The hand holding hers fondled her fingers lightly while he watched her with those unexpectedly light eyes for a moment. Not completely averse to being charmed in other circumstances, Sara kept her mind firmly on more practical matters for the moment, and managed to extricate herself without making it too pointed.

'I presume you've come for the jug,' she said, and Giovanni Cantorini shrugged carelessly, making it obvious that he would have preferred to dwell on more interesting matters.

'If you please, Signorina Sara, though you are far prettier.'

His mock humility made her uncomfortable; she was not accustomed to such fulsome flattery, and those steady, speculative hazel eyes were alarmingly disturbing. Seeking activity as a distraction, she laid the jug on its side and rolled it carefully in tissue before handing it to him.

'Did you know it was a reproduction, Signor Cantorini? Your father didn't believe me when I mentioned it, but it's true.'

'Then of course I believe you, *signorina*!'

'You didn't question the amount I paid you, so I assumed you knew.'

'You gave me enough for my immediate needs.' The

17

hazel eyes sparkled at her wickedly in the yellow shop lights as he carelessly took the package from her. 'I am not an expert in such matters, I am concerned only that they are there to be sold when I cannot persuade Carlo to give me more money.'

Such a calculating view shocked Sara, who had an admiration for the ancient treasures she handled that almost amounted to reverence, and she shook her head at him reproachfully. 'Oh, but you shouldn't feel like that about the beautiful things of the past! They can never be made in the same way again, they're unique.'

It was startling to realise how involved she had become with a complete stranger, but her subject was very dear to her and she liked to think that everyone shared her feeling to some extent. Giovanni Cantorini reminded her of just how involved she had become when he leaned over the counter towards her, the Bologna jug abandoned and apparently forgotten for the moment.

Perhaps he took her desire to interest him in antiques as simply a means of getting to know him better, for her hand was seized in slim brown fingers that curled around hers where they lay on the glass-topped counter, and his eyes glinted at her with unmistakable meaning, so that her pulses fluttered a warning that things were going much too fast for her.

'But I am delighted by beautiful things, Signorina Sara, it is simply that I prefer them to be alive and very female.' Once more his lips were pressed to her fingers and he was smiling directly into her eyes. 'You know my meaning?'

'I know your meaning, Signor Cantorini, but I think it would be better if we stuck to the matter in hand. I just hope for the sake of my reputation that you haven't got the idea you can do the same thing again and get away with it.'

'Oh, but of course not!' He reached into a pocket and produced the required amount of lire, then added several more to the pile, smiling at her look of surprise. 'You will have less difficulty explaining the transaction if you have a profit to show to your uncle, hmm?'

It was true, and maybe he deserved to be made to pay for his wrongdoing, but Sara had made a promise to his father that she would sell it back at the price he paid, and she would keep her bargain. 'That isn't necessary, Signor Cantorini. I promised to sell back at the same price, and I shall keep my word.'

Sara, could all too easily recall that stern dark face glowering at her from the other side of the counter and refusing to pay her a profit to recover his own property, and she adamant, shaking her head firmly. 'But, *signorina——*'

'I don't go back on my word, *signore,* and I made a promise.'

It looked for a moment or two as if he was going to argue the point, but it was obvious that he still had other matters in mind, and he shrugged resignedly after a while and thrust the extra lire carelessly back into his pocket. '*Molto bene,*' he said, then reached for her hand again. 'There are more important things to talk about, hmm?'

'I have a business to run, *signore.*' Her reluctance to dismiss him surprised her, for she had never imagined herself being influenced by such blatant flattery. Yet Giovanni Cantorini affected her in a way she had never experienced before, and she was not as resistant to the sensations he aroused as she felt she ought to be. 'I—I have to get on, if you'll excuse me.'

'You will not talk with me?'

The hazel eyes were appealing and alarmingly affecting, so that she was uncertain whether it was relief or annoyance she felt when a shadowy figure outside in the street suddenly evolved into a client, preceded by the jangling of the door bells. Giovanni Cantorini's reaction was quite plain, for he made no attempt to hide it, but Sara hastily released her hand from his and half smiled at the man who came across the shop towards her.

'Good afternoon, can I help you?' She glanced at the slightly sulky look on her first caller's face and smiled uneasily. 'If you'll excuse me, Signor Cantorini. *Arrivederci!*'

'I will see you again, be sure of it!' He seized her hand, making her gasp in surprise, and under the slightly bemused gaze of the new arrival, conveyed it to his lips. '*Buon giorno, signorina!*'

'*Buon giorno.*'

She was aware of the newcomer's barely concealed interest, and regretted the flush that coloured her cheeks as she gave him her attention. Giovanni Cantorini, it seemed, did not intend being dismissed from her life and, bewildered as she was by the speed of events, she thought the idea pleased her.

CHAPTER TWO

SARA's new aunt by marriage had also been her uncle's assistant in the shop, and while the honeymooners were away he had arranged for his wife's young nephew to help Sara. Crispino Vincenti was sixteen years old and very anxious to learn about antiques, so that he had no objection at all to being started at the bottom of the ladder by dusting, wrapping packages and running errands. He did it all with a touching eagerness to please, as well as occasionally lending his aid with Italian clients who spoke little or no English.

It had also been arranged that Sara should lodge with the Vincentis while she remained in Venice, and this too had worked out very well. The family welcomed her warmly, and Cris had taken it upon himself to be her escort to and from the shop each morning and evening, guiding her through the maze of narrow streets that was Venice.

She realised suddenly that he was looking across at her inquiringly, his dark eyes darting briefly to the watch that encircled his wrist. 'Shall I close the shop, Signorina Ramson?'

Checking with her own watch, Sara nodded and smiled. 'Oh yes, please, Cris. I didn't realise it was quite so late.' It would have been difficult not to notice the swift anxious look he gave through the glass panel as he hurried across to lock the door before a late client arrived and delayed their departure further, and she hazarded a guess at the reason for his haste. 'Have you got a date?'

'Oh no, Signorina Ramson!'

His hasty denial reminded Sara that it was unlikely to be so among the well brought up girls of Cris's acquaintance, but she had yet to accustom herself to the slightly more formal code of behaviour observed by most Italians where their young women were concerned. Nevertheless, seeing Cris's faintly pink colour she felt certain his anxiety to leave was in some way connected with a girl, and her smile quizzed him.

'But you expect to see someone, eh, Cris?'

He was a good-looking youth, dark-haired and dark-eyed like most of his compatriots, but not in the least brash or leeringly over-confident. His manner was grave and very adult for his sixteen years, and he was always impeccably polite, so that Sara felt rather mean for having teased him when he was so obviously embarrassed by it.

Smilingly she sought his forgiveness. 'I'm sorry, I shouldn't tease you. It really isn't fair of me.'

'Oh no, please do not apologise, Signorina Ramson, there is no need.' He hesitated, long enough to make it obvious that he had something else in mind to say. 'In a way you are right, you see.'

'You mean you *are* meeting a girl?' She laughed, giving him no time to confirm or deny it. 'Well, it's perfectly all right, Cris, I won't give you away.'

'I am not exactly meeting her.' His self-consciousness was touching and it was obvious that he felt certain she would not understand. 'You will not like what you hear, *signorina.*'

'Why not try me and see?'

Encouraged by her smile, Cris went on, though he did not look at her while he spoke. 'There is a young lady,

22

she attends the school that we pass on our way to my home——'

'The convent school?' Sara looked at him doubtfully, remembering the demure-eyed girls she had seen emerging from the school gates each evening as they passed. Some of them were sixteen or seventeen years old, but still outwardly schoolgirls. 'Isn't that rather asking for trouble, Cris?' she ventured, and Cris's dark eyes were instantly defensive.

'A glance only, Signorina Ramson! It does no harm.'

'No, I suppose not.' An incurable romantic, Sara smiled, suddenly feeling every one of her twenty-four years when she thought of Cris's romantic idol. 'But you'll either have to miss seeing her this evening or go on without me. I've still got the books to make up before I leave.'

It was clear that he was torn between the duty of escorting her safely home as he usually did and losing the sight of his *amante*, or leaving her to make her own way home, and his dark gaze flitted between Sara and the street outside for a moment or two. Almost inevitably it was duty that eventually won, and Cris shrugged resignedly as he walked back across the shop.

'Then I will stay and wait for you, of course, *signorina*.'

'Oh no, you won't!' Sara smiled at the vaguely surprised way he looked at her, and waved him back towards the street door. 'You go ahead, Cris, and let your mother know that I'll be a little later than usual, though I'll be in plenty of time for dinner.'

'But, Signorina Ramson, if you——'

'Go on, shoo! Let me get on with my book-keeping. Nobody's going to kidnap me between here and Ruga

23

Parco—you go ahead and see your girl, Cris.'

He hovered near the door, shifting his dark eyes from her to the floor of the shop, a faint flush still showing below the golden tanned skin of his face and neck. 'I swear to you that we—I have no more than smiled at her, *signorina*; a glance, that is all.'

'Then off you go and smile at her.'

His eyes were warm and velvety soft as he smiled across at her from the doorway and she wondered what there was about Italian dark eyes that was so irresistible. '*Tante grazie, signorina, grazie.*'

'Oh, Cris!' He turned back quickly, the door already open, and his eyes were anxious briefly, as if he feared she might already have changed her mind. 'I wish you'd call me Sara; I am sort of family, after all.'

Obviously taken by surprise, he stared for a moment, then a wide smile beamed across his dark young face like a lantern, showing healthy white teeth. '*Si, si! Tante grazie, Sara! Ciao!*'

'*Ciao*, Cris!'

She smiled to herself for a moment or two after he left, and hoped he would be in time to see his little convent girl. A glance only, he had said, but she had already begun to notice just how meaningful a means of communication a mere glance could be from expressive Italian eyes. But, as Cris said, there was no harm in it.

It was another fifteen minutes before Sara left the shop herself, and she glanced at her watch as she locked the door behind her. It was later than usual, but she still had plenty of time to get home before the evening meal was served, and Signora Vincenti was no stern stickler for time.

It was growing dark, but there was a velvety blueness in the sky still above the domes and spires of Venice's rooftops, flushed with a golden haze drawn from the heat of the day and hovering like a gauze among the churches and *palazzos*.

The little *campo* outside the shop was shadowed by the buildings that surrounded it, already further into night than the sky above it, but busy with people either going home or on an evening's pleasure. Just across the little square and on the right was the first of the many narrow streets that would eventually bring her to the Vincenti home, and she approached it fairly confidently, convinced she could find her way among the arched bridges that spanned the spider-web of canals.

She had been walking for some time and had taken several more turns before it began to dawn on her that she was no longer sure of her direction. With Cris to guide her she had not really needed to know the route they took, and the maze of small streets, criss-crossed with bridges and canals, began to look alarmingly alike when she emerged from one narrow *calle* to find herself confronted with a choice of three directions.

Thinking the one to the left looked vaguely familiar, she took it, almost sure she recognised the richly orna-mented face of a *palazzo* part way along. But Venice was a veritable treasure house of palaces, and it took her only a little while to realise how very easy it was to become completely lost.

Panic fluttered briefly in her breast and was hastily quelled as she turned to retrace her steps. She thought she had gone wrong after that last turning, so perhaps the safest thing to do was to go back to that point and take a different direction.

Her passing the first time had not gone unnoticed by a group of young Italians walking together, possibly on their way from work, and seeing her returning in their direction they greeted her with loud enthusiastic wolf-whistles. Her hair, free of the ribbon that tied it back during working hours, swung about her face and instead of the loose cotton smock she wore a blue dress that fitted closely enough to an excellent figure to show it to advantage.

Her admirers showed noisy appreciation of the fact. Rolling their dark eyes, they passed comment among themselves, laughing and making extravagant gestures that left their meaning in no doubt. It was not the first time it had happened since she arrived, nor, she supposed, would it be the last, but it was not easy to assume the same cool air of composure as she had the last time.

Suddenly realising that she was probably completely lost in a strange country, her composure deserted her, and she felt frighteningly alien, her heart thudding hard in her breast. Her legs felt strangely unsteady and she wished with all her heart she had not been so understanding of Cris's romantic daydreams.

Even back at the point where she thought she had gone wrong, she felt no more confident of choosing which of the two ways open to her as the right one. Choosing the direct route, straight ahead, she was faced with a hump-backed bridge that looked just like all the other hump-backed bridges, it seemed, and she climbed the approach steps with no idea of whether or not she was right, for nothing on the other side looked at all familiar.

It was getting darker all the time too, and lights glittered all along the canal, their brightness doubled by their own images reflected in the water. If Sara had been in the mood to appreciate it, it was beautiful. The mingling of day and night had a kind of breathless excitement in this city of enchantment.

Boats scuttled back and forth, the only kind of transport possible in a city that was carved into a maze of islands by more than a hundred and fifty waterways, and it occurred to her suddenly that the obvious way to get to her destination was by water. She could board a *vaporetto*, the Venetian equivalent of a bus, and be driven as near as possible to her destination.

All the time she stood on the bridge, trying to make up her mind, people were passing her. Some hurrying, some obviously in no hurry at all, but out for an evening's enjoyment. Having just about made up her mind to take a *vaporetto*, she almost cried out in alarm when a hand touched her arm lightly and a vaguely familiar voice spoke from just behind her.

'Signorina Ramson?'

Sara turned swiftly and with a wildly thudding heart as she looked at the man who had accosted her. There was no mistaking his identity, even though he was evidently not completely sure of hers. After that brief, light touch on her arm he had stepped back a pace and now stood with one hand in the pocket of his coat and the other resting on the parapet of the bridge while dark and undisguisedly curious eyes studied her quite openly.

A pair of dark trousers hugged closely to lean hips, and flared over his shoes, and a light jacket was worn carelessly open over a dark silk shirt, open at the neck to show a brown throat and the first glimpse of a tanned chest. Carlo Cantorini was not an easy man to forget, but it was his anger that was so indelibly imprinted on Sara's memory, and she was instantly wary of him. Not that he looked angry at the moment, only curious.

'Signor Cantorini!'

He showed no surprise at her addressing him by name. No doubt he knew his son well enough to realise he would have confided that much to her. The strong aristocratic face bore no trace of a smile and to Sara he was not exactly the most reassuring person she could have wished to see in her present situation.

'You appear to be lost, *signorina*.' He took the fact for granted, evidently, for he did not ask it as a question. 'I observed you from some distance away, undecided which direction to take. Perhaps I may assist you?'

Sara's first instinct was to deny that she needed assistance, but it was growing later all the time and she hated to think of Cris's mother becoming anxious because she thought she was lost. In view of what had happened at their last meeting, it wasn't easy to swallow her pride and admit that she could use his help, but she managed it somehow.

'I'd be grateful if you'd tell me how to get to Ruga Parco, please, *signore*.'

He must have known how she felt, she thought, and wondered why he had bothered to stop and offer his help when yesterday he had seemed convinced she was not only dishonest but stupid too. He seemed quite determined to be of assistance today, however, and his fingertips just lightly touched her arm once more as he turned her about.

'I can do better than that, *signorina*. Please come with me.'

She had little option but to do as he said, and he guided her back across the bridge to a narrow walk that ran alongside the canal and led eventually to a stone jetty where a motor launch was moored. She would somehow have visualised him being driven wherever he went, but there was no sign of anyone else in the launch and he helped her aboard himself with a large hand under her arm to steady her against the gentle swaying of the craft.

It was the equivalent to offering someone a lift in a car anywhere else in the world, Sara thought, only somehow she felt much more vulnerable standing beside him in the sleek shiny motor launch as it purred out into the busy canal.

'You live in Ruga Parco, *signorina*?'

'I'm lodging with some relations of my uncle while I'm in Venice. They live in the Ruga Parco.'

It was difficult to keep her voice as steady as she would have liked, but he was probably only making the inquiry as a matter of polite interest. She found him a disturbing man, even when he was not angry, and she wondered what there was about him that was so disturbing. He wasn't good-looking, not the way his son was, and she could imagine him cruel, even savage, if he was driven too far, and yet there was a magnetism about him that she found herself responding to without fully realising she was doing so.

It had not been quite so apparent when she saw him in the shop, or perhaps she had simply not recognised it, for if she thought back he had had a pretty devastating effect even then. She had been angry and indignant at the time and she had perhaps not fully appreciated just how much the character of the man himself had affected the way she felt.

She cast a wary but searching glance at him from the

corner of her eyes while he concentrated on taking the launch through the evening traffic on the canals, finding herself intrigued with the sheer physical masculinity of him.

The silver-grey flashes in his dark hair scarcely showed in the artificial light that now predominated, but instead of looking younger without them his strong dark face only seemed more fiercely stern and unrelenting, and Sara felt a small shiver of sensation slip along her spine without quite knowing what caused it.

Obviously her study of him drew his attention, for he turned his head after a moment or two and looked down at her. His dark eyes were turned glitteringly black by the lights and seemed to be questioning her interest, almost as if he found it suspect.

'Is something troubling you, *signorina*?'

'Oh no, nothing at all!'

He glanced at the lights all along the canal, shimmering reflections in the water giving a magical effect that was enchanting. 'You enjoy Venice at night?'

Taken by surprise, Sara glanced uneasily at the strong dark hands on the wheel of the launch, then at the face of the man beside her. 'I've never really seen it before, *signore*. I've only been here four days and I haven't been out at night much, and never on the water like this.'

'You have no interest in our city?'

It was curious how everything he said to her seemed to sound so much like a challenge, and for the first time it occurred to her to question her own trust in coming with him. She had not for a moment stopped to reason a motive for his offering to drive her home along the canals instead of simply giving her directions as she asked. And she should, if she considered it seriously, be far less ready to trust herself to him than to those light-hearted young men who had whistled after her in the street.

'I think your city's beautiful,' she said. 'It's just that I haven't found the time to do any sightseeing yet, but I will.'

'I hope so, *signorina*, especially since you are interested in the ancient arts of Venice.'

Once more Sara sensed a challenge behind the words, and she was tempted to respond to it by raising the matter of that controversial jug that had been the cause of their meeting. Instead she managed to sound far more composed than she felt as she changed the subject, carefully avoiding an answer that could start the controversy all over again.

'I—I hope I haven't brought you out of your way, *signore*.'

Broad shoulders shrugged carelessly beneath the light jacket. 'Very little, *signorina*. I was on my way home.'

'Oh, I see. I thought perhaps——'

She stopped herself just in time from being embarrassingly indiscreet. She had not imagined him as one of the working population, but saw him as probably on his way out for the evening, though the way he was dressed precluded a formal occasion. For all her haste, he obviously suspected her train of thought, and turned again briefly.

'You do not believe me?'

'Yes, of course I do!'

He shrugged, and Sara wished she might feel more cool and confident. Her slightly breathless air was bound to convince him that she was no older than his son, and as he took them under another bridge, giving wide berth

31

to a slower moving gondola, he spared her another brief glance.

'Are you in the habit of accepting lifts from strangers, *signorina*?'

He sounded so much like a stern parent that Sara flushed, looking up at him swiftly. 'No!'

'And yet you allowed me to persuade you.' He gave her no time to find reasons, even if she could have produced them, but went on, lecturing her coolly and quietly, as if he had every right to. 'You are a very pretty girl and my countrymen are rather more bold in their admiration than your own, I think. You would do well to take more care, Signorina Ramson.'

The comment on her being a pretty girl was hardly a compliment, she told herself, merely a statement of fact, and she wondered how he came to be so short of the kind of romantic boldness he claimed for the rest of his countrymen. She was, she knew, less worldly than most of her contemporaries, thanks to her restricted upbringing, but she was no naïve child to be advised against the dangers of romantic Italians, and she thought it was time she put him in the picture.

'You really have no need to warn me, Signor Cantorini. I'm quite old enough to walk around Venice alone without coming to grief.'

'Really?'

A faint but distinct overtone of amusement in the deep voice was enough to bring a flush of burning colour to her cheeks, and she rolled both her hands tightly about the catch of her handbag. She had not imagined him with a sense of humour, and the fact that she was the butt of it made it worse, though she tried to keep her composure rather than quarrel with him in the present situation.

'I think you're probably under the impression that I'm younger than I am, *signore*. It's a mistake that quite a few people make until they know me.'

For a moment the dark gaze was switched to her again, scanning her flushed face, with the grey eyes huge and brightly shining in the reflected lights on the water. Her mouth was set as firmly as she was capable of making it, but still looked soft and remarkably vulnerable, and she caught a glimpse of a brief, sardonic smile before he turned away.

'You look very much younger with your hair like that, *signorina*, and without that loose garment disguising your shape.'

He turned his head for only a moment, but in that time the blue dress felt as revealing as if it was made of gauze, with dark eyes noting every detail with an explicitness that stunned her. Shaking from head to foot in a way she could not control, she did not even notice that he was bringing the launch in towards the bank until he spoke again, in the same matter of fact tone.

'This is as close as I can bring you, *signorina*. The rest of the way we must go on foot.'

Sara was startled for a moment to realise she was actually home at last. The distance she had to go on foot was no more than a few steps, for she recognised the little balcony garden of the Vincenti home even from below, and stared up at it for a second as if she found it hard to believe she was really there.

The launch was swiftly moored and a large hand reached down to help her on to the steps that led up to the street, Ruga Parco, where she lived. Standing on the top step for a second or two trying to find suitable words to thank him, she realised suddenly that Carlo Cantorini had no intention of simply being thanked and dismissed. That light feathery touch was still on her arm, and it was clear from the faintly inquiring expression on his face that he meant to accompany her right to her door.

'I'm very grateful to you for bringing me home, Signor Cantorini, thank you. I'll be fine now.'

He seemed much taller suddenly and she realised that he was standing much closer than he ever had before, so that their bodies were in contact and not just that light touch on her arm. A very slight inclination of his head gave a curious suggestion of intimacy too and Sara felt her senses responding in a way that startled her.

'Naturally I will walk you to your door, *signorina*.'

'There's really no need.'

Heaven knew why she was making such an issue of it, for the gesture was natural enough for a man like Carlo Cantorini, she knew. The fact was she felt curiously shy of being seen with him, for if Cris or any of his family was to see her with this tall, autocratic stranger for an escort, heaven knew what ideas they might get, and she wondered if mentioning the fact might deter him.

'I—there might be one of the family looking out for me.'

The light hold on her arm tightened only fractionally, but it was enough to tell her that he followed her train of thought well enough and was not deterred. 'It shows that someone cares for your safety, *signorina*. That is well.'

'I just didn't want to—to embarrass you. In case they get any wrong ideas,' she added hastily when she sensed the dark eyes looking down at her.

'That troubles you?'

Sara glanced up swiftly, then down again as they drew nearer the lighted windows of the Vincenti house. 'Not really,' she admitted, and was almost surprised to realise it was true. But even after only four days with the family, Signora Vincenti had left no doubt that she could not understand an attractive girl of twenty-four still being single, and she did not want any misunderstandings.

At the moment there seemed little she could do to discourage him, so she walked beside him the short distance to her lodging feeling a curious and unfamiliar flutter of excitement in her breast. The door was ajar, as if they had either seen her coming or someone had slipped out for a moment, and she put out a hand and pushed it wider before turning to renew her thanks. A small tremulous smile was on her mouth.

'Thank you, Signor Cantorini.'

Taking her hand was an unexpected move that startled her into catching her breath audibly, but he merely shook it very formally and then released it, leaving the impression of his strong hard fingers on her flesh.

'I have to thank you for returning the Urbino, *signorina*. My son told me that you refused to take the extra money he offered for its return.'

'I told you I was honest, *signore*, but you found it hard to accept—I hope now you're convinced.'

'And you feel entitled to an apology, do you not?'

Sara hadn't been going to press that point, but apparently he was bent on making full restitution for his mistaken opinion of her. 'I don't——'

'Very well, Signorina Ramson, I apologise for doubting your honesty. Does that satisfy you?'

'Yes, of course, but——' She looked up at him in the harsh yellow light that flooded out from the house windows and hesitated. 'I do wish you'd believe me about the jug, Signor Cantorini. It isn't a genuine Urbino, it really isn't.'

'We shall see.'

The short non-committal answer was curiously unsatisfactory and despite her need to hurry if she was not to miss dinner, Sara pressed further to convince him. 'I know my antiques, *signore*, and I promise you I know what I'm saying.'

'It remains to be seen.' The dark eyes held hers for a moment with such intensity that she shivered and hastily looked away. 'I think that you will agree I must seek the opinion of someone else in the matter.'

'Naturally, though I'm not as inexperienced as you evidently think me, *signore*.'

'No?'

He spoke softly and there was an inflection in his voice that suggested quite a different kind of inexperience, so that Sara's face flushed warmly as she tilted her chin, her grey eyes bright and wary. 'Thank you for bringing me home, Signor Cantorini. I really must go in now or someone will be looking for me. *Arrivederci!*'

The last thing she saw before she turned and walked into the lighted hall was Carlo Cantorini's dark head inclined in a brief bow, and she did not look back, no matter how tempted she was to do so. She did not even turn when she recognised Cris's footsteps coming across the tiled hall behind her, hurrying to catch up with her.

He managed it just as she started to climb the stairs to the first floor rooms where the family lived, cool and airy, overlooking the canal she had just driven along with her unexpected escort. 'Sara?' Cris watched her face as he climbed beside her and she could guess that he had seen Carlo Cantorini leaving; he must have done.

'Hello, Cris, did you think I'd got lost?'

He had a bottle of wine tucked carelessly under his arm and she savoured the idea of it with whatever it was that smelled so good in Signora Vincenti's kitchen. 'You were so late that we thought something must have happened to you, and Mamma has scolded me for leaving you to come home alone.' He glanced back towards the now closed door and flicked his dark brows meaningly. 'I see now why it is that you are so late.'

Nervously sensitive, Sara shook her head firmly as they walked along to where she had her room. 'I did get lost, in fact, Cris. Heaven knows where I went wrong, but I must take more notice next time we walk to the shop, and make sure I know the route. I lost my way completely.'

'But you were rescued, huh?'

No wonder he could carry on a no-touch courtship with his little convent girl, Sara thought ruefully; he could put a whole world of meaning into those expressive dark eyes of his. It was not possible to say nothing, and she had no real reason to feel so touchy about being rescued by Carlo Cantorini, but somehow she drew back from the only possible interpretation Cris and his family were going to put on the incident.

'You remember I told you about the Bologna jug yesterday? The one I tried to convince its owner was a reproduction and he wouldn't believe me?'

'*Si, si,* but——'

'That man was the owner of the jug and he recognised me when I was standing on one of your lovely but all-alike little bridges trying to think which way to go next. He brought me home in a motor launch.'

'So!'

It was there again, that knowing and very disconcerting look in his eyes, and Sara shook her head. 'Signor Cantorini was simply being polite to a visitor to his city, Cris, so you can take that look off your face!'

She put a hand on the knob of her bedroom door and stood for a moment, drawn by his rapid and startling change of expression. 'That was Signor Carlo Cantorini?' She nodded, and Cris rolled his expressive eyes heavenwards, shaking one hand loosely and making curious moaning noises through his teeth. 'Oh, Signorina Sara, you are how is it—in the lion's den, eh?'

It was obvious that he would arouse her curiosity with something as provocative as that, and Sara stared at him for a moment and frowned, her need for haste forgotten for a moment. She had seen Carlo Cantorini as an austere man in his relationships as well as in business, and what Cris was saying did not fit in with that conception at all.

Even his attitude towards his son had seemed to suggest family pride rather than warmth, and Giovanni Cantorini had declared his father no charmer of ladies, as he put it. Despite that rather disturbing magnetism and a certain aura of sensual power, she could not imagine him a ladies' man, although—— She shook her head hastily.

'What on earth are you talking about, Cris?'

Cris's dark eyes had a wicked gleam in their depths and he was laughing to himself as he turned and walked off with the bottle of wine under his arm, winking at her over his shoulder. 'Signor Carlo Cantorini has a—how is it?—a reputation, eh?' He winked an eye and laughed once more, shaking his head and making much of his meaning. 'You will do well to take care, Sara!'

'Cris!' He stopped and turned once more, looking back at her with that teasing gleam still in his eyes, the wine bottle held by its neck and resting on one hip. 'How do you—how *can* you know so much about him?'

For a moment he regarded her more seriously, then he smiled once more and lifted his shoulders in a slight shrug, as if he had convinced himself that she had no more than a passing interest in the man they were discussing. 'I read the newspapers, Sara.'

'He's been in the newspapers?'

'*Si*, quite often he is in them; pictures too. I did not see him very close just now, so that I did not recognise him, but I have seen him very often.'

'Gossip columns!'

What she felt for such items showed clearly in her voice, but Cris was shaking his head to deny it. 'No, Sara. There is no *comàre*, only reports of his being here and there.' His dark eyes twinkled wickedly at her and once more that fluttering lid suggested far more than words could have done. 'It is Mamma who—how is it you say?—reads between the lines, huh?' He shook his head at her just before he turned away, waving the wine bottle and tossing the words carelessly over his shoulder as he went off. 'She calls him a breaker of hearts, so have a care, Sara, or——'

He went off, half running along to the family living-room where his mother was waiting for the wine, and his laughter gave Sara a curiously uneasy feeling in her stomach.

CHAPTER THREE

IT was another two days before Sara heard anything more of the Cantorinis, though they were not forgotten by any means. Both men had made much too strong an impression on her for her to forget them easily, although it was Carlo, the elder one, whose personality had made the strongest impact.

She had to admit that she had found Carlo Cantorini a curiously disturbing man, and it occasionally surprised her to realise just how clearly she could recall his strong, autocratic features and the shadowed darkness of his eyes. She could not deny that she was curious about him, intrigued even, not mentioning him again to Cris was not a good idea, she thought.

It was bound to give rise to speculation if she asked about the newspaper reports Cris claimed to have read. Just how Signora Vincenti had become an authority on reading between the lines, Sara had no idea, or how Carlo Cantorini earned his reputation as a breaker of hearts, as Cris had dubbed him. But no matter how, probing was out of the question, for she found Cris's dark eyes much too discomfiting, looking as they had two nights ago when he learned the name of the man who brought her home.

She was making an entry in the sales book with her mind only partly on what she was doing when the door-bells jangled suddenly and she looked up. Her automatic smile becoming less certain when she saw who it was that came walking across the shop towards her beaming his wide, confident smile to show how certain he was of his welcome.

'Ah, *buon giorno*, Signorina Sara!'

Knowing that Cris was in the back room unpacking some newly acquired stock made her glance instinctively over her shoulder. The concealing curtain hid the open doorway, but it allowed anyone behind it to hear most of what was said in the shop. She wasn't even sure whether or not she was glad to see Giovanni Cantorini again, but knowing that Cris was there, within hearing, made her horribly self-conscious, so that she greeted the newcomer with very formal politeness.

'*Buon giorno*, Signor Cantorini.'

It wasn't quite the welcome he expected, evidently, for a small trace of a frown flitted across his good-looking face. But she could almost sense Cris listening now that he had heard the name of Cantorini, though he probably had the father in mind at the moment rather than the son.

Giovanni himself was, as yet, unaware that they were overheard and he leaned against the glass counter as he had last time, his body inclined slightly towards her in a posture that conveyed a suggestion of intimacy, and gave Sara a disturbing little niggle of apprehension in the pit of her stomach.

The smile lent warmth to his hazel eyes too, and he reached to take her hand before she could anticipate him. He held her gaze steadily, then raised her hand to his lips in a gesture that fluttered a response from her senses. For all his youth he was a practised charmer.

'So formal, Signorina Sara! When we have been so—involved as partners in crime together!'

'The crime was yours, *signore*, not mine!'

He obviously had a taste for the dramatic, but Sara found herself with a strange desire to laugh suddenly without being quite sure why she felt as she did. He looked at her reproachfully, as if he felt genuinely hurt by her response, and it gave him a boyish look that he was probably unaware of.

'Like many beautiful women, you are cruel,' he accused, and his fingers tightened for a moment to let her know he did not like her reception of him. 'It is not a crime to take what will one day be mine. If it had been so, Carlo would have let you call in the *polizia*.'

'I hardly think so, in the circumstances.' She did not know why she felt so sure, but she could not think of Carlo Cantorini calling in the police to deal with his son's misdemeanour. He was, she felt certain, a man who would deal with that sort of incident himself. 'I think you know that quite well, *signore*.'

'*I* know Carlo, *bella mia*, you do not!'

Easing away her hand, Sara bent again over the sales book, her voice firm and leaving him in no doubt how she stood from now on.

'I hope you haven't come to sell me anything this time, *signore*. I really can't afford to become involved in another disagreement with your father!'

'You *are* still angry!' He sounded so surprised that Sara wondered if he had any idea of the trouble he had caused her.

'I'm—wary, Signor Cantorini. You made things very difficult for me the last time, and they could have been worse if I hadn't placated your father by promising to return the jug to you.'

'But have I not said that I am sorry?' The hazel eyes were so appealing when she glanced up at him that she

42

regretted having been rash enough to look up. 'Please believe that I mean it sincerely, *signorina*.'

'All right.' She tried to keep at least half her attention on the sales book, because it seemed the safest thing to do somehow. 'I accept that you're sincere, but I can't change my mind about not taking anything else you bring in to sell.'

'I have nothing!' He spread his hands, dramatically exposing their emptiness. 'And now that you have been proved right in the matter of the jug being a reproduction too, will you not agree to let the whole matter be forgotten between us?'

Sara stopped writing and stared at him. Her grey eyes were wide and almost wary, as she sought confirmation. 'Did you say it's been confirmed that the jug was a reproduction?'

'*Si*. Carlo had an expert give his opinion, and he confirmed that it was as you said.'

'Well!'

Sara sighed her satisfaction, her grey eyes bright with the pleasure of being proved right; but Carlo Cantorini should have come with the news himself and told her; indeed, she found it hard to believe that he had delegated the task to his son. He had not struck her as that sort of a man.

'I hate to say I told you so,' she said to Giovanni, 'but as I insisted when I saw Signor Cantorini the other night, I *do* know my job, no matter what his opinion of me.'

It was a moment or two before he fully realised the implication of what she was saying, and when he did he looked at her, frowning curiously. 'The other night?' he queried. 'You have seen Carlo since he came to make you give back the jug?'

It was then she realised he knew nothing about her being lost and driving home with his father, and seeing the look in his eyes was almost as discomfiting as the knowing gleam she had seen in Cris's. She was reminded again of Cris too, and knew for sure that he would be far more interested in the conversation going on in the shop at the moment than he was in getting on with the task she had set him to do.

'Oh, I got lost on my way home a couple of evenings ago.' She tossed off the information with a casualness she was far from feeling, and shrugged carelessly. 'I left later than usual and without Cris to show me the way I got myself lost.'

'Cris?'

She could imagine the ears listening to every word behind that concealing curtain, and shrugged. 'The boy who works here—my uncle's nephew by marriage, actually. He went on ahead and I got myself completely lost without him. Signor Cantorini, recognised me and drove me home in his motor launch.'

'And said no word about it to anyone.' The fact seemed to be significant to him, and he was smiling in such a way that Sara felt a flush of colour in her cheeks as she hastily avoided his eyes.

'I'm not surprised—why should he? It was hardly very important, although I was very grateful to him for coming to help me.'

Giovanni's eyes held a glint of mockery, as if he knew exactly how she was feeling, and his smile seemed to make a lot more of the episode than she liked. 'Oh, Carlo can be very gallant when it pleases him to be, but please do not be misled by his helping you, Sara, he is a very practical man.'

Sara had no idea what he implied by that rather enigmatic comment, but she preferred not to go further into it at the moment, and she shrugged again lightly, realising that the gesture was becoming rather a habit, albeit a useful one. She returned to her book-keeping again, though her pen merely hovered above the page for the moment.

'I imagine he must be, since he took the precaution of having the jug authenticated.'

Giovanni nodded, not much interested, she suspected, in the outcome of the matter. Antiques, he had freely admitted, meant little to him. But he was a determined charmer, and sufficiently astute to recognise what he considered an attractive girl behind the severe hair-do and the shapeless smock she wore in the shop.

He took the pen from her unresisting fingers after a second or two and laid it on the counter, then held her hand in his while he looked deep into her eyes, with his elbows resting on the glass top. His voice was low and just slightly unsteady, so that she felt a little shiver of sensation slide along her back when he spoke.

'I am much more interested in you, *bella* Sara, than in those wretched old pots that Nonno and Carlo hold in such high regard.' He squeezed her fingers lightly, his gaze steady and inescapable. 'I came to ask you to have dinner with me, will you do this?'

'Oh, I don't know.' The instinct to refuse out of hand was almost irresistible, and yet she could not quite understand why it should be so. In part, she supposed it was because she knew Cris could hear what was being said and she felt self-conscious, but also she found it hard to

45

commit herself to anything concerning either of the Cantorinis. 'I don't think it would be a very good idea, though I'm flattered that you asked me.'

'Then why do you refuse me?'

It was a reasonable enough question in the circumstances, Sara supposed, and yet she hesitated to answer it. 'I don't honestly know why,' she confessed after a second or two, 'except that I don't think your father would like the idea very much.'

It was true. Sara could imagine that stern autocratic face being marred by a frown at the news that his son had been seen dining in public with an English girl from an antique shop, though she was probably doing him an injustice when she attributed such a snobbish cause to his objection. He would probably object just as firmly to a wealthy Italian girl, if she was someone he did not know and approve of.

Giovanni was watching her with the same hint of challenge she had recognised in his father, only he was so much younger that the effect was less disturbing. 'You think that Carlo would not like it if I took you out?' he asked, and to her horror Sara flushed.

'Only because you don't know me and you're——'

'You think me too much a boy, perhaps?'

His eyes glinted resentment, suggesting that the matter of his youth had only recently been a subject of discussion, and he held tightly to her fingers while he looked into her eyes. He might be young, but his anger could be pretty formidable, she guessed—he was that much his father's son.

'I didn't say that, I——'

'I am almost twenty years old, Signorina Ramson, and I am no schoolboy, I can assure you! If you come to

46

dinner with me, you will see that I am not!'

'I didn't suggest you were, Signor Cantorini——'

'Gianni! Have I not asked that you call me Gianni?'

'Very well—Gianni.'

'*Bene!* Now will you not also change your mind about having dinner with me?'

In his anxiety to persuade her he leaned further across the counter towards her, but in doing so his elbow brushed against a Bohemian glass tankard displayed on a small shelf that stood on the counter top. It was a mere touch, but sufficient to topple the lightly balanced tankard, and Sara reached out hastily and anxiously to catch it, conscious as always of how easily precious things could be broken.

'Oh no!'

Her cry carried despair, and instinctively Giovanni responded to it, turning round a second later to try and catch the tankard before it crashed to the counter. He was too late and his reach was more urgent than accurate, so that instead of serving the purpose it intended, his hand struck Sara's face instead just as she bent her head.

In a moment Cris appeared in the curtained doorway, his wide dark eyes taking in the scene as he saw it. The tankard now stood on the counter, unharmed, but Sara was holding a hand to one side of her face and shaking her head, while Giovanni Cantorini made soothing noises and tried to apologise profusely in Italian. It was not at all as Cris imagined it, but he was not to know that, he only knew what he saw. The man in the light suit had obviously struck Sara in the face, and whether or not he was now sorry about it, made no difference.

'Sara, are you badly hurt? I will call the *polizia*—please to stay where you are, *signore!*'

47

It was clear that he meant to protect her, and his concern was so touching that Sara felt almost unkind for telling him it was unnecessary. He obviously thought her in dire need of his assistance, and he had come to her aid without hesitation. Giovanni was looking so stunned by his sudden appearance so soon after the incident that Sara hastened to speak up.

'It's not necessary to call anyone, Cris, really! Honestly,' she insisted when she saw the doubt in his eyes. 'Signor Cantorini and I both grabbed for the tankard as it fell and his hand accidentally caught my face instead, that's all.'

Cris regarded the already darkening mark just under her left eye with some doubt, and he frowned at Giovanni fiercely. 'It is as well that I am here, Sara, is it not?'

'I'm very glad you're here.' She spoke truthfully, for she thought she could rely on him whoever had been there and whatever the situation. Smiling, she reached out and touched his cheek lightly with a finger-tip. 'Thank you, Cris, but it was just an accident.'

Still distrustful, he peered at her face and frowned. 'Should you not have a doctor to see your hurt, Sara? You will have a bruise very soon, and perhaps some——'

'I'm all right, Cris, really.'

'*Benissimo.*'

He shrugged and withdrew to the back room once more, but it was clear from the frown he gave Giovanni that he was far from happy about leaving them together, and Sara found his concern very touching. Not so Giovanni, for he was looking at the concealing curtain suspiciously and scowling.

'I did not know that we have another person here

48

while we speak, Sara. I must take care when I call to see you!'

Inevitably Cris would have heard him, and Sara could imagine his good-looking young face flushed and indignant. He was only a year or two younger than Giovanni, but there was a world of difference in their outlook and their upbringing. Although she had no way of knowing it, she suspected Giovanni Cantorini was an only child, while Cris had five sisters and a brother, all older than he was and married. He was much more of a boy, for all his fierceness in protecting her.

'I'm living with Cris's family while I'm in Venice,' she explained. 'I don't know what I'd do without him, both here in the shop, and walking me home every day.'

'Except when you leave late and Carlo finds you lost!' The dig had been too much for him to resist, she realised, and could only hope that Cris had not taken it too much to heart. 'It seems that Carlo has a better sense of occasion than I have, Sara, and that saddens me.'

It was clear that knowing Cris was there in the back room inhibited him to some degree, and he was no longer quite so bright and confident as he had been when he came in. He seemed more vulnerable and unsure of himself, so that Sara actually began to feel sorry for him. She need not have troubled herself, however, for he recovered sufficiently after a few moments to smile at her once more, though rather less beamingly.

'I am very disappointed that you will not come to dinner with me,' he told her. 'We would have much to talk about. My mother was English, did you know that?'

'No, I didn't.'

In her brief speculation on what Carlo Cantorini's wife would be like, she had never taken into account the fact that she might not be Italian. Certainly it had not occurred to her that she would be English, for apart from his hazel eyes, Giovanni was so very Italian.

She noted the use of the past tense too, so presumably Signora Cantorini was dead, which would explain the reputation her widower had acquired for himself, if Cris was to be believed. In some curious way Sara found it a relief to know there was no wife in the background to be hurt by what he did, or was reputed to do.

As he sensed her interest, Giovanni's smile resumed a little of its previous confidence, and he leaned both elbows on the counter once more, taking care that there was nothing he could damage. 'That surprises you, hmm?' He looked at her through his lashes, his confidence growing every second. 'I would like to tell you about her, and about me too. Does that not tempt you, Sara?'

There was little use denying it, for he must know she was intrigued, but she still hesitated, even though she smiled at him as she shook her head. 'I don't think I should have dinner with you simply because I'm curious,' she said, and he laughed.

'Then come because I want you to, eh?'

She was weakening and she knew it, so did he. There was no real reason why she should not go with him. He was several years her junior, but that was not such a barrier at their ages, and he looked so much older than his nineteen years, just as she looked younger than her twenty-four. The idea of dining out with a good-looking escort in the romantic setting of Venice was eventually irresistible, and she gave in at last.

'All right.' She laughed, as if she did not quite believe she was agreeing after all, and wondered what Cris thought of her lack of resistance. 'I'll have dinner with you, Gianni. Tonight?'

He hesitated. Only the merest fraction of a second, but she noticed it and would have said something had he not hurried on before she could speak. There was a hint of breathlessness in his voice as he laughed and took her hand again, and she eventually put it down to excitement, though taking a girl to dinner was not likely to be a novel experience for him, she thought.

'*Si, si*, tonight, Sara! I will fetch you at seven, eh?'

'All right—at seven.' She could sense Cris once more, on the far side of that concealing curtain and felt self-conscious suddenly. 'Do I need to be very formal?'

As he had a moment ago, Giovanni hesitated, though why was as much a mystery as before. 'Not unless you wish to be. We will go to some small, quiet place, hmm? Where we will be alone and unobserved.'

'Unobserved?'

Sara felt a curious twinge of misgiving for a moment, but his laughter soon dispelled it, and he shook his head until his dark hair fell across his brow and he brushed it back with an impatient hand. 'I am well known around Venice, *bella* Sara. We will have no privacy if any of my friends see us, and I wish to be alone with you.'

It was still so difficult to see him as half English, and she smiled over it while he held her hand, so that he quizzed her with his dark brows, curious to know what was amusing her. 'I find it hard to believe you're partly English,' she told him. 'You're so very Italian, Gianni.'

'It is true.' He kissed her fingers lightly, his hazel eyes gleaming with mischief in his darkly good-looking face. 'I will tell you about my mamma.'

'I'm intrigued!'

'I am enchanted!' He kissed her fingers again. 'We shall enjoy our evening, *bella mia*, I promise you.'

It was much too late for her to think Giovanni Cantorini would come for her now, and Sara felt a cold weight of disappointment in her stomach, as well as humiliation. From across the room Cris looked at her from time to time with his solemn dark eyes, and did nothing to ease the way she felt. His pity was an expression she both hated and appreciated, but it made her feel like crying, and that was something she would not do.

Somehow she had known, deep in her heart, that this would happen. When Giovanni Cantorini had spoken of taking her to a small place where his friends would not see them together, she should have realised what lay behind his desire not to be seen with her. He had hesitated when she suggested they meet that night; that should have been clue enough. He had not expected to be pinned down to a definite date, but she had not even thought about that.

For more than half an hour now she had sat and waited for him to come for her, and the pale green dress she had felt so right in initially felt much less glamorous than when she first put it on. It was long and it clung closely to the softly feminine curves of her body and, though it was lower in the neckline than she normally would have worn, she felt it was the kind of thing that Giovanni Càntorini would like.

The toe of one green shoe poking out from below the hem of her dress tapped impatiently and she was beginning to think it was time she went and changed. Something more plain and everyday that would dispose of this unfamiliar glamorous image as a dismal failure. It was only pride that kept her there, flicking through the pages of a magazine that she could not even read because it was in Italian.

Signora Vincenti was sorry for her, just as Cris was, but she had not expected things to be just as Sara anticipated, not when she knew she was seeing Giovanni Cantorini. The fact that she had been let down badly was not unexpected, but was none the less sad for all that and she felt it with almost as much anguish as if it had been one of her own daughters.

'I am sorry, *signorina*.'

Sara looked across at her; small and plump and so contentedly homely with the last of her big family beside her, and she shook her head, managing a smile as she did so. 'Oh, it's my own fault, Signora Vincenti. I should have known better than to make a date with someone like Giovanni Cantorini.'

'He will be a man like his father,' Signora Vincenti prophesied gloomily. 'A breaker of hearts; you may be sure of it, *signorina*.'

'Is he?' Curiosity overtook disappointment for a moment. 'Has Carlo Cantorini such a terrible reputation, *signora*?'

Her plump shoulders shrugged, and Signora Vincenti's dark eyes had a doleful rather than a condemning look as she answered. 'It is wrong always to blame the man in these affairs, *signorina*, but there have been so many women in the life of Carlo Cantorini, and never a marriage since the first one.'

Incredibly, Sara found herself seeking excuses for him. He was a widower, so she believed, and there seemed no moral reason why he should not escort as many women as he wished. 'I can't see anything wrong in that, *signora*. He is a widower.'

She knew her hostess was unlikely to see eye to eye with her, but she was unprepared for the tight-lipped look of disapproval that her defence brought to Signora Vincenti's homely face. 'With a son to whom he should set an example, *signorina*! But Carlo Cantorini is a man of amusement only—not one who takes a wife as he should and has more sons! That is not good!'

So that was it. Sara almost laughed at the little woman's indignation. She frowned on the idea of a man like Carlo Cantorini seeing so many different women instead of marrying one of them and settling down as a family man. It was the Italian image of family life and children that made her so disapproving, not necessarily because she considered him immoral, and Sara found it hard to understand her own sense of relief.

'Perhaps he had enough of marriage with his first wife,' she suggested. 'Did you know she was English?'

Signora Vincenti looked vaguely disbelieving. 'This I did not know, *signorina*!'

'Giovanni told me she was.'

Signora Vincenti pulled a face and shrugged her plump shoulders. 'How does one believe such a man?'

Sara had no chance to voice her belief, for her heart gave a sudden urgent leap in her breast at the sound of the door bell in the hall downstairs. Maybe it was Giovanni after all, or maybe it wasn't, but either way she was given no opportunity to find out for herself, for Cris was already on his feet before she even had time to stand up.

'I will see who it is!'

He was half way through the door before she could

speak, and she heard his footsteps on the stairs, scurrying quickly, as if he half expected her to follow him. Seconds later there were voices in the hall, then silence, and Cris's footsteps coming back; alone still, so whoever it was had not come up with him.

Neither Sara nor Signora Vincenti said anything while they waited, but Sara had her hands curled tightly on her lap. Somehow, from somewhere, she recognised the voice in the hall speaking to Cris, and it was not Giovanni Cantorini. But she was almost certain it belonged to his father.

Cris was breathless from hurrying, his dark eyes bright and inquisitive, and both women watched him. He glanced first at his mother, then gave Sara a short, keen survey before telling her who it was down there in the hall.

'Sara, there is Signor Cantorini to see you.' He paused, as if giving her time to prepare for the bombshell. 'Signor Carlo Cantorini!'

Sara's heart was thudding hard as she got to her feet, trying to appear cool and calm when she felt quite the reverse. She had recognised his voice in the hall, but nevertheless having Cris confirm it was startling, and she could not imagine why he was there unless—— She caught her breath on the possibility of his being responsible for Giovanni's non-appearance, but then wondered if he would have come to tell her.

'You will see him, Sara?'

Cris's question drew her back to a level of consciousness, and she blinked at him vaguely for a second or two before nodding her head. 'Yes, of course I'll see him, Cris. There's probably a very good reason why Giovanni hasn't come, and maybe his father will tell me what it is.'

'Ah, *si*!'

It was pretty clear from the look Cris exchanged with his mother that he doubted very much if explanations were the reason for Carlo Cantorini being down in their hall waiting for Sara to join him. He said nothing, however, but merely shrugged, and, murmuring her excuses, Sara left them, closing the door carefully behind her.

Normally it stood open in the summer, but she remembered how easy it had been for her to recognise the caller's voice when he spoke to Cris, and she shrank from the idea of her conversation with him being overheard, however involuntarily.

Even this early in the evening a light was necessary in the hall, for it was virtually windowless and always dim and cool. A bronze lamp hanging from the centre of the ceiling was the only illumination. It used very little electricity, but it left the outer edge of the hall almost in darkness so that from the staircase it looked as if there was no one there.

Sara looked around for a second, wondering if he had had second thoughts and left again. But then, from the shadows on the far side, a tall figure stepped into the yellow light as she came down the last few steps and she felt her heart suddenly thudding in her breast like a drum-beat.

He wore evening dress, which took her momentarily by surprise, until she recalled the time of day. Dark trousers fitted closely to lean hips and long muscular legs, and a white dinner jacket made his dark features look almost dusky in contrast; a silk shirt with a frilled front was an unexpectedly flamboyant touch with those

56

autocratic features but suited him perfectly. He was every bit as disturbing as she remembered him, and the steady scrutiny of his dark eyes was enough to make her hastily look away as she went to meet him.

'Signorina Ramson.' He took her hand and raised it briefly to his lips, but did little more than brush her fingers before he let it go again. From his superior height he looked down at her and she felt more conscious of the slight discoloration under her left eye than she had since it happened. 'You have hurt yourself?'

Instinctively she touched the spot, a short and dismayingly unsteady laugh making light of it. 'Oh, it was an accident. It looks much worse than it is really.'

'I have to apologise to you once more, it seems.'

She was so nervous and uncertain that for the moment she forgot that Giovanni had let her down by not coming for her, and she shook her head hastily. 'Oh no, that really isn't necessary, *signore*, it was pure accident!'

A frown drew black brows together for a second and he gazed down at her in obvious disbelief. 'I do not quite follow you, *signorina*. Is there any reason why I should apologise for your face being bruised?'

It dawned on her then that he had something quite different in mind when he apologised, and she felt the colour flood in to her cheeks as she was overcome with embarrassment. 'I'm—I'm sorry. No, of course, you don't have any reason to apologise—I—I misunderstood you, *signore*.'

He would not leave it there; she should have known, of course, he was not that kind of man. In the soft yellow light his dark eyes scanned her flushed face, seeking other bruises, other imperfections on the smooth skin.

'Am I to understand, Signorina Ramson, that my son is responsible for that—disfigurement?'

Sara would not have put it nearly so melodramatically, and she shook her head quickly from side to side, anxious to convince him that Giovanni had not deliberately struck her, as it seemed likely he suspected. 'It was an accident, *signore*. A glass tankard was in danger of falling and I bent to catch it at the same time as Gianni—Giovanni reached out to save it.' She shrugged, as if it was all perfectly straightforward and understandable. 'I caught the tankard and he caught his hand on my face.'

For a moment she wondered if he believed her, but then he was inclining his head in a brief and very formal bow, and his mouth had a tight, straight look that she found incredibly discomfiting. 'Then it seems I have yet another reason to apologise to you, Signorina Ramson.'

In view of her own initial response to him, his formality struck her as almost chilling, and she looked down at a spot somewhere about half way down the frilled front of his shirt rather than meet his eyes, her honey-gold hair swinging forward in a silken curtain to hide her face from him.

'You really have no reason to apologise at all, *signore*.'

'I cannot believe you mean that, *signorina*!'

Impatience edged the deep voice and seemed to confirm her opinion that he was not a man who suffered fools gladly. She had suspected he might be behind his son's non-appearance, but she had not expected him to appear in person and admit it. Somehow it was adding insult to injury if he had, and she looked up at him at last with a bright challenging gleam in her grey eyes.

'Unless it's because you put your foot down firmly on the idea of Giovanni taking me to dinner! That had crossed my mind, though I admit I find it hard to believe anyone would be so—so feudal in this day and age!'

The sudden hardening of those strong dark features, and the glittering resentment in the almost black eyes when they looked down at her for a second before he replied, made her tremble. His nose was Roman in its arrogance, and he held back his head so that he looked at her down its impressive length.

'It seems I have already been condemned, *signorina*, so there seems little point in my explaining! I beg your pardon for intruding upon your time; please excuse me!'

'Oh no, please!'

Reaching out her hand and putting it on his arm the way she did was an impulsive move, and she immediately withdrew when he turned and looked at her once more with that disconcerting steadiness. Clasping her hands together in front of her, she pressed her bottom lip with her thumbs and looked at him anxiously. No one had ever made her feel so nervously inadequate before, but Carlo Cantorini seemed to have the knack of doing it each time they met.

'I'm sorry, *signore*, I must have misunderstood. I shouldn't have spoken out without stopping to think, but——' She spread her hands in a gesture of appeal and shook her head. 'I've been waiting for Giovanni for more than half an hour, and I——'

'You are angry, of course.'

He seemed to accept the fact as natural enough, and his own anger had apparently evaporated as quickly as it had been aroused. He was not an easy man to anticipate, and for a second or two Sara tried to control the response of her senses as he stood facing her under the yellow hall light that cast softening shadows over his dark face.

'You know—did you know that Giovanni was supposed to be taking me out to dinner tonight?'

'*Si*, I knew. That is why I am here, *signorina*.'

Sara frowned at him curiously. 'I assumed you came to tell me that you didn't approve of him dating me,' she confessed, and wondered if she had been so very wrong in that estimate after all.

His dark eyes travelled slowly over her slim shape in the clinging green dress, lingering at the place where the neckline plunged to show a shadowy vee of creamy skin, and Sara remembered the last time he had looked at her like that. Then, as now, the dress she wore seemed very inadequate and she felt suddenly and alarmingly vulnerable.

'You know little about me, Signorina Ramson, or you would know that I do not command my son's social life. He may take out whomever he pleases within reason, but even he is not allowed to date two in one evening.'

'Two?' Sara glanced up quickly and caught a brief glimmer of that slightly malicious humour she had noticed before. 'You mean I wasn't the only one he made a date with?'

Carlo Cantorini was nodding agreement, and she noticed how those intriguing flashes of silver above his ears seemed to catch the overhead light. 'I am afraid so, *signorina*. Giovanni already had an appointment to dine with someone else when he made that date with you and, while I do not normally interfere in his social arrangements, I felt in this instance that I must.'

'Yes, naturally.' She thought she knew what was coming, and was surprised to find herself less troubled by Giovanni's double dealing than she had been a short time ago.

'Signorina Laurana is an old friend,' he went on, apparently bent on letting her down lightly. 'She is a friend of childhood, you understand. We have known her family for many years.'

And she was a much more desirable companion for his son, Sara thought, getting the picture quite clearly. 'Yes, of course I understand, Signor Cantorini. I'm grateful to you for coming to see me and explain.'

'*Un momento, signorina.*' The deep voice broke across her words before she had quite finished speaking, and she looked up at him again with a curious fluttering sense of excitement she could do nothing about. 'I do not think you do understand. Since Giovanni cannot take you to dinner, I am offering myself in his place. Will you have dinner with me, Signorina Ramson?'

CHAPTER FOUR

IT all still seemed a little unreal to Sara. She had started the evening by anticipating a pleasant meal with Giovanni Cantorini, but she had foreseen nothing like this happening, and she knew with certainty that she would not have felt the same way about being with him as she did with her present companion.

A small quiet place was what his son had promised her, but the reverse was the case with Carlo Cantorini, for the huge and richly ornate restaurant had probably changed little since the days when it was a palace. Furbished with baroque splendour and agleam with gilt and elegant long mirrors that reflected the dazzling light of crystal chandeliers, it was like something out of a dream, and Sara revelled in it.

Most of her life had been spent appreciating the beauties of past ages, but tonight she felt she had been plunged into the very heart of the past itself. She could imagine this splendid palace peopled with Venetian nobles and their families, giving great banquets and buzzing with talk and laughter, just as now, and she felt a kind of breathless thrill at the glimpse of past greatness it afforded her.

She could still be surprised at finding herself in the company of the tall, autocratic man who sat opposite to her too. Carlo Cantorini was an attentive escort; lacking his son's flamboyance, but with a quiet self-confidence that suggested a man accustomed to getting exactly what he wanted, when he wanted it. He was just the kind of man to accompany her dream of Renaissance splendour.

He had ordered *risi e bisi* for her with no more than a briefly raised brow to seek her approval, but she enjoyed the delicious soup and its accompanying rice and small, tender green peas so much that she had quite happily left the choice of the rest of the meal to him. Scampi had never tasted so good, and it seemed almost sacrilegious to follow tender veal in a delicious wine sauce with anything more than a fresh peach.

Sara enjoyed every mouthful, and her expression left no doubt of her enjoyment as she sipped from her wine glass and watched the people around them with a slightly absent air of satisfaction. She was fully aware of being scrutinised herself, and she wished to avoid looking at her companion for the moment, for he was much too observant.

The wine was cool and sweet, but more potent than she had anticipated, and she felt strangely relaxed and slightly lightheaded. It was a dangerous combination in the present situation, she supposed, though so far she had little reason to suspect Carlo Cantorini had anything in mind other than giving her dinner.

'You have enjoyed your meal?'

The formal and customary *signorina* was omitted, Sara noticed, and turned to look at him with a flutter of sensation curling in her stomach. 'Yes, thank you, *signore*, it was wonderful. I don't remember when I enjoyed anything so much.'

Above the white dinner jacket and soft silk shirt his tanned features appeared duskily dark, short thick lashes half concealing the gleaming darkness of his eyes. It was so difficult to see him as the father of someone as adult and sure of himself as Giovanni, and she wondered how old, in fact, he was.

He must have been very young when he married his English wife, and it probably explained his subsequent aversion to repeating the experience. There was a half smile on his more usually stern mouth as he looked at her, so that Sara hastily snatched herself back from speculation and gave him her attention.

'So you have not been too disappointed with your evening after all, hmm?'

'Oh no, definitely not, *signore*!'

She sounded much too breathlessly naïve, she knew it, and he was bound to find it vaguely amusing. '*Bene*,' he said softly. 'I am thankful that you do not take Gianni too seriously.'

Anxious to reassure him, Sara shook her head firmly. 'Oh, I'm not likely to do that, Signor Cantorini! He's only nineteen, after all.'

'Ah, *sì*!'

She had been right, he did find it amusing, and she felt a flush colour her cheeks as she looked at him across the table. She did not want to do anything to spoil their perfect evening, and yet she felt compelled to let him know once and for all that she was not as young as he obviously took her to be.

'I'm twenty-four, *signore*; five years older than Giovanni, and a good many more than that in maturity, I suspect!'

'Indeed, *signorina*?'

She refused a cigarette with a shake of her head and he lit one himself, bending his head over so that she saw the strong features at a curiously distorting angle for a second or two, and shivered when she felt a cold touch along her back, like the caress of an icy finger. Looking up once more, he held her uncertain gaze with narrowed dark eyes.

'You find my son too immature for your taste, eh?'

Heaven knew what she had let herself in for by making that impulsively malicious comment on Giovanni's character, but it was beyond recall now and she could only try and revise the impression she had given. Her fingers toyed restlessly with the stem of her wine glass, her hair falling forward like a silky curtain to hide her expression from him when she bent her head.

'I'm afraid you misunderstand me yet again, *signore*. It's simply that I don't take Gianni seriously, as you said.' She looked up suddenly, forgetting for the moment that he probably knew the young man they were discussing better than anyone did. 'He isn't nearly as worldly-wise as he appears at first, he can look quite—vulnerable.'

Carlo Cantorini's dark gaze held hers steadily, slightly narrowed behind the curl of blue smoke from his cigarette. 'You are very observant, Signorina Ramson. You now perhaps understand my indulgence in the matter of his taking the Urbino—*scusi*, the reproduction Urbino jug.'

Thankful of a distraction from the subject of his son, Sara grasped the opportunity to change it. 'Gianni told me that you had an expert to examine it.'

'And he proved you to be right. *Si*, that is so, *signorina*. It was to make recompense for my doubting you that was partly responsible for my asking you to have dinner with me.'

'I see.'

Once more that challenging dark gleam taunted her from across the table. 'That surprises you, *signorina*?'

'No, not really.' She could truthfully admit that, for she had believed he would apologise sooner or later, though not quite so extravagantly. 'I knew—I guessed you'd tell me yourself.'

'I think that I am flattered by your trust, *signorina*!' The dark eyes gleamed like jet in the yellow light overhead. 'Now the matter may be forgotten, hmm?'

'Yes, of course.' She drank the last of the wine in her glass, then glanced at her wristwatch and laughed, a light and faintly unsteady sound when she recognised how late it was by her usual standards. 'Good heavens, I'd no idea it was that time already!'

There was a faint smile about his mouth that troubled her, for it suggested mockery, as if he suspected a strategic move to end the evening, and he regarded her for a second or two through the smoke from his cigarette. 'In Venice one does not hurry a meal, Signorina Ramson, the night is to be enjoyed. However, if you are bored——'

'Oh, but of course I'm not bored!' She flicked an anxious glance around her, fearing their conversation might be overheard and misinterpreted. 'I simply meant that—well, that it's much later than I realised, that's all. I'm not normally a night bird.'

Explaining herself, she realised too late, could only make him think her more naïve than ever, and she felt the warm colour in her face as she looked down hastily at her empty glass. Her first estimation of him had suggested a hint of cruelty in his make-up, and his present manner seemed to endorse it. From the slightly crooked smile on his mouth to the glittering mockery in his eyes.

'If it is your wish, then we will leave, of course.'

Sara saw no point in denying it, so she simply nodded

silently, and he turned to signal a waiter to bring their bill. While he was paying it she slipped away to the cloakroom for a moment, needing some time to recover her composure. She had not meant it to come to this, but he was the most disturbing man she had ever met, and quite beyond her experience.

Needing preoccupation, she renewed her lipstick, looking at her reflection thoughtfully for a moment. It was amazing what a difference it made when she freed her hair from the rather severe style she wore in the shop, and wore a more sophisticated dress, but even so she did not look her full twenty-four years. Usually it did not bother her, but tonight, somehow, it did.

She looked beyond her own reflection suddenly, aware that she was being watched, and saw a woman standing some distance behind her, using a comb on an already immaculate hairdo. Sara felt sure she didn't know her, and yet there was something about the scrutiny, something rather disturbing.

She was Italian, almost certainly, with that glossy black hair and smoothly tanned skin, and she was elegantly and expensively gowned in a cream silk creation that must have cost a small fortune. Yet there was such a look of raw emotion in the dark eyes that Sara instinctively shrank from it.

What she had done to earn such a look from a complete stranger was beyond her, but a vague uneasy suspicion was already stirring in her brain as she put the top back on her lipstick and turned from the mirror.

By the time she turned the woman was gone, and only the still swinging door showed that she had ever been there; that and the lingering smell of some exotic perfume. For a moment or two Sara stared at the door, her heart beating just that little bit too fast, and for no good reason that she could think of, then she too walked back through the swinging door and emerged once more into the restaurant.

Their table was quite near the entrance, and she suffered a brief moment of stunned surprise when she saw that Carlo Cantorini was no longer sitting there, but then she saw him, already standing in the entrance hall amid the baroque splendour of gilt mirrors and crystal chandeliers, with his dark head angled in that same arrogant way as he listened to a woman who spoke to him with agitated urgency.

The same woman Sara had noticed in the cloakroom only a few moments ago. That dark resentful stare was now explained and Sara's own suspicions confirmed. It seemed incredible that anyone as seemingly self-possessed and sophisticated could suffer jealousy, and yet it was pretty clear that jealousy had been at the bottom of her resentment, as it was the cause of her present urgent insistence.

A breaker of hearts, Signora Vincenti had called him, and it seemed all too possible that she was right, judging by the cool and almost callous indifference with which Carlo Cantorini regarded the woman who was addressing him with such urgency.

He seemed almost as if he sensed Sara's reappearance, for he turned almost at once, while she was still hesitating about whether or not to catch his eye or stroll across in their direction. A few words and a brief and very formal bow, and he left the other woman to come across and join her.

His progress was watched with bright angry dark eyes, and for a second Sara wondered if she would follow him and create a scene right there in that elegantly splendid reception hall. It would probably have been less of an ordeal to a volatile Italian, but Sara shrank from the very idea, and she heaved an inward sigh of relief when the woman eventually tossed her head and made her way back into the crowded restaurant.

'I hope I didn't interrupt anything,' she began when he joined her, but he simply gripped his strong fingers about her arm and led her out into the night, without offering a word of explanation.

It still intrigued her that there was no motor traffic in the city of Venice itself, and she was increasingly attracted to the idea of either walking wherever she went, or taking one of the busy little *vaporetti* that plied constantly to and fro on the canals, or a *motoscàfo* that could be hired much as a taxi was hired on dry land.

It only needed a moon to be perfect, she thought as they walked out into the street, and nature had been kind enough to provide even that. It sat like a round yellow lamp in the deep purple sky, scattering silver coins over the surface of the water and making magical silhouettes of the domes and spires on the skyline.

Even in her wildest dreams, Sara had never imagined herself living anywhere like it, and she sighed quite involuntarily as she walked with Carlo Cantorini beside her over one of the innumerable small hump-backed bridges that crossed and re-crossed the maze of canals. It had never been mentioned that they should do other than walk, but she had been in favour of the idea after the meal they had eaten.

'Something troubles you, *signorina*?'

The soft-spoken inquiry snatched her back to reality. 'No, *signore*, I just—sighed, that's all.'

She could well imagine that rather sardonic smile without looking up at him; it was reflected in his voice. 'But this is not the Bridge of Sighs, Signorina Sara, though I have no doubt that it has heard the sighs of many young women on nights such as this.'

The implication was clear enough to bring a sudden flutter to her heartbeat. Carlo Cantorini was no doubt used to walking home in the moonlight, but to Sara there were too many romantic settings in Venice, and too many opportunities to become entangled in situations she could not cope with. It was a dream world, not to be taken seriously, but with the kind of magic that made it impossible to do anything else.

On the other side of the bridge it was shadowed and silent as they walked into a narrow *calle*, not much used and with long black shapes looming in from either end where the lamps cast the shadows of tall buildings before and behind them. Carlo's hand on her arm had tightened its hold slightly, though she had been unaware of it happening, and she found herself much closer to the lean warmth of his body as they walked along the dark *calle* towards another brightly lit waterway, and another small bridge.

Perhaps if her brain had been less clouded by the wine she had consumed earlier, she might have seen danger in the situation, but as it was she felt only a strange kind of awareness that fluttered like a moth inside her. Coming suddenly out into the Ruga Parco stunned her for a moment because it was so unexpected, and something of her reaction must have been transmitted to Carlo Cantorini.

He looked down at her and smiled—not the slightly mocking smile she was used to seeing, but one that warmed his eyes and showed a glimpse of strong even teeth in the darkness of his face. 'You are surprised to find yourself home, *signorina*?'

Sara nodded. She had to admit to a sense of disappointment too, which was oddly disturbing in the circumstances. 'I—I hadn't realised we were that close.'

'You wished to come home, did you not?'

She hadn't, Sara thought, though it was by far the wisest thing to do after the amount of wine she had drunk at dinner. The narrow street was shadowed, even with the lights of the tall houses streaming out into it from either side, but there were places that the lights never reached—small alleyways, so narrow that they were in semi-darkness even in the full light of day, and Carlo Cantorini stopped beside one of these, drawing Sara with him into its shadowy darkness where the walls of the houses felt chill to her bare skin.

'I have brought you home as you wished, Signorina Sara, hmm?'

There was a softness in his voice, a thrilling depth that had an effect on her senses that she could do nothing about, and she felt herself trembling when he leaned towards her slightly, with his dark eyes discernible only as glittering orbs in the shadows. It was impossible to keep her own voice steady and controlled.

'I've enjoyed my evening, Signor Cantorini, thank you.'

'So?'

The soft-voiced inquiry both mocked and soothed, and she felt herself responding to it in a way that startled her. She must keep that woman back there in the restaurant firmly in mind, as well as Signora Vincenti's prophecy. Heartbreaker he might be, but so far there was still time to keep her own heart intact.

'It's—it's very late, *signore*, I really should go in.'

A small, impatient sound with his mouth showed how he felt, but as yet he did not move and she felt incapable of pushing him out of her way. 'Must I apologise once more? For keeping you out when you would seek your bed early like a *bambina*!'

The deep voice mocked her, making her clench her hands tightly at her sides. 'Please don't speak to me like that, Signor Cantorini!'

She was aware of him with every nerve in her body, and it stunned her to realise how much she wanted to reach out and touch him. There was a fierce, sensual masculinity about him that was almost tangible as he stood only a breath away looking at her with his glittering eyes, and she remembered how she had seen him as a man who got exactly what he wanted, when he wanted it. The night air was warm, so warm that it was like silk on her bare arms and shoulders, and yet she shivered.

'Are you sure that Gianni is so much too young for your taste, *signorina*?'

There was a harshness in his voice, a rough depth that brushed her sensitive nerves until she shook her head from side to side to deny him the right to affect her like this. 'Signor Cantorini——'

'Carlo! My name is Carlo!'

'Carlo.'

She repeated his name obediently and breathlessly, leaning back against the wall behind her because her legs were suddenly too weak to hold her. She scarcely knew him, it was too soon to let him go on like this, and yet there seemed so little she could do to stop him.

His hands on her shoulders had a caressing firmness

and she caught her breath, moving her head in an agony of helplessness when they brushed aside her honey-fair hair before he bent and pressed his mouth to her neck. It was a light, gentle caress, but at the same time there was an urgency in the touch of his lips that stirred an alarming response in her.

The most disturbing part was that she wanted him to kiss her. It was almost beyond her control not to respond to him with all the fervour of a woman in love, and yet it simply wasn't possible that she could be in love with a man she had met only twice before. His mouth brushed warmly against her throat and the soft rounded line of her jaw, until his breath hovered above her parted lips.

'Sara!'

In the moment when their mouths touched, a woman's laughter rippled softly on the night air, coming to them from the direction of the street, and Sara drew back swiftly, her eyes huge and dazed. Footsteps echoed along the road, and a man's voice murmured something inaudible, followed by more laughter that was suddenly stilled in the same moment as the approaching footsteps, leaving no doubt as to the cause.

'Goodnight, Signor Cantorini!'

She slipped out of his arms before he even realised what she meant to do, and hurried the few steps to the Vincenti house which still had its lights blazing despite the lateness of the hour. A man and a woman stood just a little way along the street, much too preoccupied to notice her, their arms locked around one another, their bodies so close that they made one dark shadow against a wall, and Sara felt a sudden and inexplicable twinge of envy.

It was quite instinctive that she looked back the

second before she stepped in through the doorway, and she saw the tall figure of Carlo Cantorini striding away from her along the lamp lit street, looking even more lean and virile with a suggestion of anger in the briskness of his stride. Her legs still shakily unsteady, she watched him disappear in the direction of the little bridge they had so recently crossed, but he did not turn his head for even a second.

No one had asked if she enjoyed her evening. Perhaps both Cris and his mother thought it more tactful in view of her flushed face and bright evasive eyes when she returned, but whatever the reasons Sara was grateful not to have to answer questions. She would simply not know how to explain her reactions to Carlo Cantorini, especially in view of their opinion of him.

Being busy helped to fill her mind with things other than the persistent memory of dark, shadowed eyes as they hovered above her, and warm breath on her lips whispering her name. If that unknown woman had not filled the silent street with her sudden laughter, heaven knew where it would have ended, for she had been ready to surrender, she knew it, and realising it both stunned and alarmed her.

'Sara?' Cris's voice brought her back once more, and she turned and smiled at him a little vaguely. It was not the first time in the past two days that she had looked at him in that curiously vague way, and Cris was puzzled. 'Do you not wish to have lunch, Sara?'

'Oh, good heavens!' She glanced at her watch and pulled a face, apologising for forgetting the time. 'I'm sorry, Cris, you must be starving.'

'I am hungry, *si*.'

They usually had lunch together at a small *osteria* quite near the shop. It was an arrangement that suited them both, and Cris was excellent company for all his youth. He talked freely about his family and his friends to her, and about Venice, which he loved with the same fervent affection that all Venetians seemed to have for their city.

They sat outside, overlooking the water, and shaded by vine-draped trellises, while they ate a dish of *antipasto* between them and sipped a glass of wine each. The variety of olives, mushrooms, eggs, etc., that would normally have been eaten as hors d'oeuvres served them as a main part of their meal, with perhaps a slice of *pizza* for Cris when he was extra hungry.

It was a pleasant way to pass a lunchtime and Sara found it wonderfully relaxing, even with the buzz of other people's conversation around them. She passed Cris the money to pay the waiter, then got up and made her way through to the street, turning to smile when she heard Cris coming up behind her.

'*Buon giorno*, Sara.'

It wasn't Cris who smiled at her, but Gianni Cantorini, and she glanced hastily beyond him to the frowning face of her youthful escort. Cris's opinion was in no doubt, for he made no attempt to conceal it. Coming to join them, he put himself between her and Gianni, his smooth young face flushed and a warning glint in his eyes.

'I—I didn't expect to see you.' She excused her lack of welcome with an uneasy smile. 'How are you, Gianni?'

Cris being there made him slightly uneasy, but he had to accept the fact that he was unlikely to leave them, so he made the best of it, though it gave a slightly defensive edge to his manner as he took her hand. 'Until I saw you smile, *mia bella*, Sara, I was afraid that you would not even speak to me.' Raising her hand, he pressed his lips to her fingers, looking at her from the shadow of his lashes. 'I am so relieved that you forgive me.'

Sara had genuinely forgotten that she had anything to forgive him for, and her expression was enough to make it clear to Gianni in the moment before she recovered herself. 'Oh, you mean about the other night?' She gave a breathless little laugh that could have fooled no one. 'Please don't worry about it, Gianni! Anyone can forget on the spur of the moment, and I did rather rush you into it!'

'No, no!' He squeezed her fingers hard, ignoring Cris's dark frown. 'I was wrong to treat you so, but I was punished for it, that must be your comfort.'

'Punished?'

Time was forgotten for the moment, and only Cris's light tug on her sleeve reminded her that they had been gone rather longer than usual already. As if by mutual consent they all three turned and walked along the street towards the shop, with Gianni somehow managing to be beside Sara and Cris on her other side, looking fiercely discouraging.

'Carlo took you to dinner, did he not?'

'Yes.'

Any more, she felt, would have given him some clue as to just what a disturbing experience it had been, and anyway Gianni was intent upon his own feelings at the moment. He kept hold of her hand and looked down at her with those incredibly appealing eyes as he kept step with her.

'That was my punishment, knowing that Carlo was with you when I had so wanted to take you myself, though I did not learn of it until afterwards.' He glanced at her from the corners of his eyes, searching her face for a second before he asked, 'Were you not disappointed, Sara?'

Making light of it, though it wasn't easy, she found, Sara shrugged and smiled. 'I was very disappointed for a while,' she admitted. 'I thought you'd simply forgotten me and left me sitting there in my glad-rags with no-where to go, then Ca—then your father turned up.'

'And took you to dinner!' He sounded quite outraged, as if it was the last thing he would expect his father to do. 'He set out only to explain to you why I could not see you after all. That was what he promised he would do, there was nothing said about him asking you to dinner!'

What impulse, Sara wondered, had prompted Carlo to change his mind? He had claimed it was in part because he wished to make amends for having doubted her qualities as an antiquarian, but it was the rest of his reason that she found intriguing. Sensing that Gianni was waiting for her to comment, she shook her head slowly and offered the only reason she knew.

'He said it was to make up to me for telling me I didn't know my job—so I suppose that's it.'

'He told you this?' Gianni frowned curiously for a moment, then shook his head. 'It is not like Carlo to apologise so—extravagantly.'

Those had been her own sentiments, but Sara did not say so. Taking the shop key from her handbag, she bent to insert it in the lock, speaking over her shoulder as she did so. 'Oh well, perhaps he just felt like going out to dinner.'

It was Cris who took the key out of the lock, following them through into the shop but making no move to disappear behind the curtain into the back room. Instead he stayed by Sara behind the counter, hovering close by with a faintly defiant look on his good-looking young face because Gianni so obviously expected him to leave them.

'Sara——' An expressive hand conveyed Gianni's feelings in the matter and Sara hesitated only a moment before smiling at Cris.

'It's all right, Cris, I can manage for a minute or two if you'd like to go and carry on with packing that glass for Mr Greig, will you? He's coming for it at three.'

'Si, benissimo, Sara.'

He disappeared with obvious reluctance, but Sara knew well enough that he would miss nothing of what was said from now on, and Gianni would not dare put a foot wrong or he would be back to join her. She did not smile as Gianni did when the boy did as she asked, but opened one of the books on the counter and ran her finger down its columns.

'Sara!' Strong fingers gripped her hand and stilled it, holding tightly until she looked up. 'Tonight I have no one else to take to dinner, and I would so like another chance to take you. Will you have dinner with me, Sara?'

Without being able to quite explain her feelings, Sara just knew that she did not like the idea of being seen in public with him when she had so recently been with his father. It was perhaps over-fastidious of her, but it was the way she felt, and she shook her head regardless of Gianni's frown.

'I don't think I could, Gianni. Oh, it isn't that I'm

holding anything against you for the other night, but——'

'I do not understand you!'

Still shaking her head, she laughed a little unsteadily as she freed her hand and closed the book on the forgotten figures. 'I don't quite understand myself,' she confessed. 'But I don't—I can't quite bring myself to be seen dining out with you after being seen with Ca—with your father. He spoke to several people there during dinner and—well, it was fairly obvious that they were curious about seeing him with me.' Once more that shaky laugh betrayed her uncertainty. 'A strange face, I suppose!'

Gianni's eyes had a deep dark look that quite unexpectedly reminded her of Carlo, and he was frowning. 'Where did you go for your dinner, Sara?'

She searched her rather bemused brain for a name and finally remembered it. 'Palazzo Lambrino, I think that's right.'

Whatever he said it was clear that he did not approve of his father's choice of a restaurant, and she looked at him curiously. 'He knew that you would be seen by most of Venice, why did he do it? *Dannazione*, why does he do this?'

'I don't see——' Sara began, but he interrupted her without ceremony.

'Sara, if we go to somewhere quiet, as I wished the last time, no one would see us, and you would not be—embarrassed, huh? *Per piacere!*'

It was difficult to refuse him as it had been the last time he asked her, but this time she had the memory of Carlo's strong dark face opposite her across the table, and the remembered warmth of his hands on her arms, and she shook her head hastily. Carlo had not wanted to hide her away either, like Gianni did.

'I'd rather not, Gianni.'

'Then perhaps lunch?' He was determined as well as persuasive. 'Tomorrow the shop is closed, hmm? You will have a free day to come with me. Oh, *màmma mia*, how can I tempt you?'

'Gianni——'

'Ah, *sì*, I know!' He took her hands in his and his hazel eyes gleamed at her in triumph, daring her to find a fault with his plan. 'You are the expert in antiques, so the thought of many beautiful antiques would tempt you, eh? *Sì, sì?*'

Unsure whether or not she followed his meaning, Sara laughed and shrugged her shoulders. She was touched by his air of excitement without quite knowing why or how. 'Well, yes. You're thinking about an art gallery or a museum?'

'Better, *bella mia*, much better! I am thinking of the Villa Cantorini!'

'Oh no, Gianni, I couldn't!' She stared at him, her eyes blank with surprise for a moment, though her instincts already urged her to accept without hesitation. 'I couldn't just——'

'*Sì, sì*, of course you could! Nonno would enjoy to have you come and see him, he always enjoys to see my girls!' He winked one eye with outrageous frankness and chuckled. 'Nonno still likes lovely *signorinas* even now that he is past eighty years!'

'But, Gianni, I can't just invade your home without an invitation.'

'I am inviting you, *bella mia*, and I know Nonno, my great-grandfather, will be delighted when he sees you.'

He was tapping his nose with a finger and his expression was a curious blend of mischief and solemnity. 'Shall I tell you why, Sara?'

'If you think it's a good reason for me accepting, then you'd better.'

'When Carlo had his so clever friend to see the jug that you so cleverly saw as a copy, he mentioned your name. Signor Brado did not know of you, *mia bella* Sara, but he knew the name of your uncle and he was impressed. Nonno then said that we must have Signorina Ramson in to examine the rest of our treasures, and Brado laughed. He said it was a good idea, especially since you were so pretty.'

Sara's heart gave a great lurch and she coped with a sudden feeling of excitement as she looked up at Gianni's smiling face. Carlo Cantorini had called in the expert, he was his friend, so perhaps—— She hastily dismissed the thought and smiled at Gianni curiously.

'Who told him that I was pretty?'

Looking down at her with his hazel eyes gleaming with mischief, Gianni smiled confidently. 'Naturally I did. That is why I claim the right to take you and show you the many things I know you will enjoy seeing. I am not so enthusiastic about such things as Carlo and Nonno, but if you will come and see them——' His fingers squeezed hers tightly and persuasively as he raised them to his lips. 'You cannot refuse me, Sara, huh?'

Sara, her heart urging her to accept, half smiled and surrendered. 'I'll come,' she said.

CHAPTER FIVE

So many times during the day Sara had second thoughts about the wisdom of accepting Gianni's invitation to visit his home. Right up until the moment when he came for her she was in doubt about going. From the moment he asked her she had been uncertain, and once away from his persuasive influence her uncertainty grew until she was almost decided to refuse after all.

She scarcely knew them, and yet during the past few days the Cantorinis had loomed so large in her life that she was beginning to see some kind of personal involvement as inevitable. She had made up her mind early on to stay clear of such involvements, but with Gianni so persuasive such a vow was difficult to keep.

Signora Vincenti's socially-minded husband was spending an evening with his friends and Cris was off somewhere on his own, so that only the Signora sat with Sara on the garden balcony, and she was quite plainly unhappy about the forthcoming visit. While Sara sat waiting for Gianni the Signora said little, but her feelings showed in her brown eyes, and she shook her head in regret when Sara recognised the launch coming along below the balcony and prepared to leave.

In response to Sara's smile and a murmured goodbye, she merely nodded solemnly, adding an admonishment as Sara went through into the house, '*Addio, signorina*—have a care!'

Downstairs in the dim cool of the hall, Gianni stood exactly where Carlo had stood only three nights earlier, and she immediately recalled him; tall and dark, and infinitely disturbing under the yellow hall lamp. It was a recollection she hastily dismissed as Gianni took her arm and tucked it with confident familiarity under his own, then closed the fingers of his other hand over hers.

He looked at what she was wearing with the same intent interest too, though his scrutiny was much less disturbing than Carlo's had been. A light blue cotton dress with short sleeves and a fairly high rounded neck gave her a demure and rather little girl look that Gianni obviously approved of, judging by his smile.

'*Molto bella*, Sara,' he murmured. 'You look very lovely.' Bending his head, he kissed her fingers as they walked out into the sunlit street. 'Blue is like your eyes!'

Sara smiled, brushing back the honey-fair hair from her face with a free hand. Why should she disillusion him if he thought her grey eyes were blue? She felt excited despite her misgivings and as he helped her into the motor launch she lifted her face to the merest breath of a breeze that rose from the water as the boat left the steps.

She had no way of knowing whether or not Carlo Cantorini would be there, and she wished she had the necessary panache to ask Gianni without giving him the wrong impression. If he was there, it was quite likely, she feared, that he did not take kindly to the idea of her invading his home. Gianni had implied, by his remarks about his grandfather, that he often took girl-friends home, but somehow Sara did not like thinking of herself as one of Gianni's girl-friends.

They passed under the balcony of the Vincenti home and she instinctively looked upwards, catching a glimpse of trailing pink roses spilling over the railings towards the water. Signora Vincenti had a great many misgivings about this visit, and Sara could almost sense her watching the launch with her troubled dark eyes as it sped along the canal.

'I am so glad that you are here.' Gianni looked down at her, speaking over his shoulder and smiling his satisfaction at the way things were. 'I was so afraid that you have changed your mind by this morning. That you have had other thoughts.'

'Oh, but I did!' Sara laughed as she admitted it, remembering how close she had come to changing her mind. 'I'd almost made up my mind I'd tell you I wasn't coming. I thought about getting in touch with you several times.'

'Ah, but you did not, that is what matters, *bella mia*!'

'Only because I didn't know how.' She admitted it with a rueful laugh and glanced at Gianni's sudden frown. 'I'm still not sure I ought to be coming with you, Gianni.'

'Oh, but of course you must!' He looked round at her and his hazel eyes were serious, as if he thought she might still have second thoughts. 'I have told Nonno that you are coming, and he is looking forward to meeting you.'

'He doesn't mind?'

'Of course he does not mind! Have I not told you that Nonno likes pretty *signorinas*?' He rolled his eyes wickedly at her and showed his excellent teeth in a wide smile. 'I am like him, eh?'

'It must be a family trait!'

He took the rather rash remark as a compliment, evidently, for he was laughing and using his very expressive features to convey delight in the idea. '*Si, si*, we are all the same!'

'All of you?' Somehow the question was irresistible, and Gianni was pursing his mouth as he considered for a moment, then shrugged his shoulders.

'Carlo maybe a little less than Nonno and me; but he is the serious mind, eh?'

Not quite as Cris and his mother had seen it, Sara mused, and wondered which version was right. Maybe a little envy coloured Gianni's view of his father's social life, and for the first time it occurred to her that maybe there was a certain amount of rivalry between them. After all, Carlo Cantorini could be very little more than seventeen or eighteen years older than Gianni, and they were both stunningly attractive men in their different ways.

'You're not really much like Carlo, are you, Gianni?'

'In the way I look? No, I do not think I am.' It was fairly clear that something she said had not pleased him, but for the moment she could not think what it was. 'You call him Carlo?'

Sara looked at him sharply, realising how easily the name had slipped out. Her heart was beating harder suddenly, and from the warmth in her cheeks she knew she was blushing like a schoolgirl, which appalled her in the circumstances.

'I—he asked me to. I thought perhaps he preferred to be called by his christian name; you call him Carlo, don't you?'

'*Si*, but I am his son.' He spoke with an edge of steel on his voice that reminded her of his father. 'He is not usually so ready to invite strangers to use his name.'

Silenced for a moment by the apparently uncharacteristic gesture and trying to find a reason for it, Sara gave her attention to the passing buildings that crowded together along the water's edge, rather than look at Gianni. If only she had kept a guard on her tongue it would not have been necessary to find an explanation, and Gianni would not be glancing at her over his shoulder as if he suspected heaven knew what.

'I can't imagine why he did it.' She tried to keep her voice as steady and matter-of-fact as possible. 'Anyway, it surely isn't important enough to make an issue of, is it, Gianni?'

For a second the good-looking young face was kept in stern profile to her, and she was once more reminded of his father by the tightness of his mouth and the arrogant tilt of his head. He kept it up for a second or two, then seemed to relax slightly, and a moment later he turned his head and pulled a rueful face at her.

'I am sorry, Sara. I do not know why I am so angry about it. It is nothing, huh? Carlo would not be so foolish as to suppose he could seduce you!'

He laughed as if the very idea amused him, but to Sara, who could all too easily remember the lean strength of Carlo Cantorini as he held her close to him, the prospect had been too close for comfort. Maybe he had had seduction in mind, or perhaps he had intended to do no more than kiss her, but whatever his intention, Sara had come much too close to succumbing to the persuasion of that firm hard mouth, and she had a curious tightening sensation in her stomach at the thought of seeing him again.

'Ecco!' With his left hand Gianni made a gesture in the direction of a tall house, set back slightly from the water and with steps and a landing stage making an opening in a low stone wall. 'Villa Cantorini!'

It wasn't quite what Sara expected, but it was more

grand not less so, and she felt a certain amount of awe as she took in as much of it as she could while Gianni brought the launch to the steps and moored it. From below the wall it was impossible to see it at all, but it came into view again when Gianni had helped her ashore and they climbed the somewhat worn steps to the arched gateway that gave access to its grounds.

In fact grounds was rather too ambitious a word to use, for it was little more than a paved courtyard of very uneven stone slabs with just a few tired-looking shrubs in ornamental tubs, that someone had neglected to water. They looked tired and on the point of dying, and it struck Sara as rather ironic that they should have died of drought surrounded by so much water.

The house itself was both tall and wide, four stories high with tall arched windows embellished with stone carving, and with two of the levels fronted by balconies from which vines of some kind hung in long tentacles as far as the floor below and casting shadowy patterns on the rather shabby walls. The whole place had a curiously rakish air of neglect, but it was impressive for all that, and Sara felt a curl of excitement in her stomach as Gianni took her across the courtyard.

Facing them was a massive wooden door which would have been enough to deter her if she had been alone; with Gianni's hand on her arm she had little option but to go on. Set in the centre of the door was a gilded cockerel's head with the beak wide open as it issued a clarion call, and Gianni pointed to it as they stood in the doorway.

'You see that we too have our symbol, Sara. You have the ram, we have *il gallo*!'

Too nervous to do more than simply nod, Sara followed him and caught an audible breath when she stepped into a huge hall. It was cool and dim and had a tessellated floor, just like the one in the Vincenti home, but there the similarity ended, for this one was much grander. From it doors seemed to open in every direction, and a long gallery ran around three of its four sides with three staircases leading up to it. The ceiling in the centre of the hall soared to the height of two whole floors and was decorated with gilded scrollwork that ran down to the walls of the gallery in great sweeps of baroque extravagance.

The grandeur of it took Sara's breath away and she looked around her with her eyes wide and unbelieving, unable to accept that people actually lived in such a place. It must cost a fortune in upkeep, and if one looked too closely some indication of the strain on the present family's finance was evident in various small signs of neglect. The first impression was one of incredible opulence, but after a moment or two the signs became apparent, and Sara thought it rather sad.

Nevertheless there were carpets on the stairs that looked in fairly new condition, and nothing suggested that there was a shortage of staff to keep the place clean, for it gleamed with good care. Her initial shock over Sara took note of the undoubted signs of an immense treasure trove gathered under the one roof, worth far more than it would have cost to restore the villa but far too precious to part with.

The paintings that hung on the walls were alone worth a fortune, and there were any number of *objets d'art* standing in niches around the vast hall and on small elegant gilt tables. It was all the more incredible to think of Gianni having no feeling for such beauty, when she considered he had been brought up in this treasure house. For herself she could imagine nothing more satisfying.

'There will be time for you to see them later,' Gianni promised, recognising her eagerness. 'First I will introduce you to Nonno—he will be waiting for us.'

'Yes, of course.'

She felt an almost sickening sense of anticipation in her stomach as Gianni led her up one of the carpeted stairways, and she knew that the way she felt was at least in part due to the possibility of meeting Carlo Cantorini again.

After the vastness of the hall, almost anything would have dwindled by comparison, but it took Sara only a moment to realise that the room they went into was at least as large as the Vincentis' hall, and probably much bigger. It was light and airy and the view it commanded made sense of living on the first floor rather than at ground level, apart from it being cooler.

Its walls were hung with more paintings, while urns and vases and some exquisite little statuettes stood in every available space around the room, reflected and illuminated by tall, gilt-framed Venetian mirrors. It was such a dazzling and beautiful room that for a moment or two its only human occupant was overlooked.

Then Gianni's finger-tip touch on her bare arm brought her from her first dazed reaction, and she realised that there was already someone else in the room, a man who rose from a deep leather armchair as they crossed the room towards him with a curiously stiff movement that at first she took to be autocratic and unbending.

He must have been well over eighty, if he was indeed

Gianni's great-grandfather, but he was tall and there were still traces of once handsome features in the hawk-like face below thick white hair. It was more apparent after a second or two that the stiffness of his gait was caused by physical effort rather than pride, and in other circumstances she would have begged the old man not to trouble getting up for her. To suggest such a thing to one of the Cantorinis was unthinkable, no matter what his age or infirmity.

'Nonno, may I present Miss Sara Ramson. Sara, my great-grandfather, Signor Giovanni Cantorini!'

He made the introduction with a flourish and added the old man's christian name with the obvious intention of letting her know that he had been named after his great-grandfather. There was very obviously a very close relationship between them, much more close than Gianni had with his father, she suspected.

'I am delighted to meet you at last, Signorina Ramson.' He raised her hand to his lips and smiled. 'You will forgive me, I hope, *signorina*, if my English is not so good as my great-grandson's.'

'Oh, but it's excellent, *signore*!' She hastened to re-assure him, laughing ruefully at her own lack of skill. 'I'm afraid I don't speak Italian at all—I wish I did.'

'Then you must mix more closely with Italians, *signorina*, and you will learn our language and give us the pleasure of your company at the same time, eh?'

A charmer, Sara thought, just like Gianni, and saw at once just who it was that Gianna most resembled. Seeing her seated, the old man resumed his own seat with evident relief, and sat looking at her with bright dark eyes, leaning back in his chair like a benevolent autocrat, for she had no doubt that he could be just as autocratic as his grandson if he felt inclined.

'Your uncle, Signor Ramson, speaks Italian, does he not?'

'Oh yes, quite well, but he's been here for some years now, and I'm only here for a few weeks.'

'Ah, you will be leaving us again?'

'I'm afraid so, Signor Cantorini, but not before I've seen much more of Venice than I have so far, I hope.'

'And of the Villa Cantorini also, *signorina*, I hope. You are most welcome to come at any time to see and examine our treasures. You would like that, eh?' It was clear from his expression that he knew just how much she would love having the opportunity of seeing the beautiful things he had in his home, and he was smiling, as if the thought pleased him. 'Consider it an open invitation, *mia cara signorina*.'

'Thank you, *signore*, you're very kind.'

'You will come?'

He seemed determined to commit her to a firm promise, and Sara could do little but comply in the circumstances. She was nothing loth to having free access to so many beautiful things, and she smiled her gratitude at the old man. 'Yes, of course I will, *signore*, thank you.'

'Ah!'

The short sharp exclamation suggested satisfaction and for a moment Sara believed it was in response to her acceptance, until she became aware that someone else had come into the room while they were talking. Half turning her head, she recognised the newcomer and caught her breath silently.

'Carlo, you know Signorina Ramson, do you not?'

The old man welcomed him warmly, a hand outstretched to indicate their visitor. It was a moment that Sara had been secretly anticipating ever since she walked through that impressive front door, but she felt now that it had been sprung on her without warning and her heart was beating hard and fast as she looked up at him briefly.

Tall, lean and disturbingly virile in a cream suit with a brown silk shirt that was open at the neck, Carlo Cantorini greeted her with polite formality, making it hard to believe that only two nights ago he had stood with her in the shadows of a small dark *calle* and held her in his arms and kissed her.

'Signorina Ramson.'

Just that, no more. Merely a repetition of her name, and Sara felt herself flush warmly. She noticed then that there was someone with him and for a second only experienced the swift urgent beat of her heart more forcefully against her ribs. The girl was much too young to be in his company for the obvious reasons, for she was no more than sixteen or seventeen, younger than Gianni, and she could not see Carlo as the kind of man who would escort a girl so much more youthful than himself.

When he spoke he addressed himself to Gianni, a fact that his son responded to in the only way he knew how. 'I saw Maria in town,' Carlo told him. 'I understand that you have promised to lend her a book, Gianni, and since I was on my way home I suggested that she came with me and collected it for herself.'

Quite clearly Gianni found the situation slightly embarrassing, but he was unfailingly charming. She was a rather pretty girl and Gianni's charm was instinctive with pretty girls. He introduced her to Sara, she obviously was already acquainted with Signor Cantorini, then looked rather smugly pleased with the fact that he had two pretty visitors.

'Am I not fortunate?' he asked his great-grandfather. 'Two beautiful *signorinas* to see me, huh?'

Instead of simply agreeing, as Gianni evidently expected, the old man glanced at the enigmatic face of his grandson. It was fairly clear that Signor Cantorini saw, or thought he saw, some devious motive behind Carlo bringing the younger girl with him, and Sara wondered how right he could be. Maybe by producing an alternative interest Carlo was making sure that Gianni did not spend too much time alone with Sara.

'Are you not going to take Maria to find her book, Gianni?' Neither Carlo nor Signor Cantorini made any attempt to see the girl seated, and obviously the old man followed his grandson's intent by suggesting that Gianni leave them. 'Signorina Ramson will be quite safe in our company for a while, will you not, *signorina*?'

Slightly unsure of herself, Sara nodded, glancing only briefly at Carlo from the corner of her eye. 'Oh yes, of course. Please don't worry about me, Gianni, I'll be perfectly happy until you come back.'

'You are sure?'

He was evidently reluctant to deprive her of his company, for he looked at her anxiously, but Sara smiled encouragement. 'Of course, Gianni.'

At least partially convinced, Gianni took the girl's arm and walked off with her, arms linked and talking animatedly in their own tongue, while Sara thanked heaven that at least the elder Giovanni was there and she was not left in the sole company of Carlo Cantorini. As the door closed behind his son and the newcomer, he sat down in the armchair next to hers and crossed one long leg over the other, regarding her with steady dark eyes for a moment before he spoke.

'Do you anticipate discovering many other—fakes among our family treasures, Signorina Ramson? My good friend Luigi Brado considers your uncle a very knowledgeable man and he is delighted that you show signs of becoming equally so.'

Sara wished she was sure whether or not he was mocking her, but the strong dark face was serious and she could detect no glimmer of amusement in the dark eyes, the few seconds that she found nerve enough to meet them. From the way he spoke he seemed to be under the impression that her main purpose in coming there was to seek out other reproductions among their riches, and she hastened to correct the assumption.

'I haven't come with the idea of looking for fakes, Signor Cantorini, only to admire the beautiful things you have—and to visit Gianni, of course.'

'Of course!'

Mockery glinted for a second in his eyes, and Sara turned thankfully to Signor Cantorini. 'I asked that you should come and see me also, *mia cara signorina!*' The old man's sharp eyes gleamed with a meaning as unmistakable as Gianni's, and he gave his grandson a brief and almost despairing look. 'Also, *signorina*, I am sure that you will find it much less confusing if you call Carlo by his name as you do Gianni; I am sure there will be no objection, eh, Carlo?'

Instinctively Sara glanced at him again and found the dark eyes on her, half hidden by lowered lids and the thick blackness of his lashes. 'Signorina Ramson already has my encouragement in that matter, Nonno, but I think she is somewhat—deterred by the informality it suggests. Is that not right, *signorina?'*

That unmistakable air of challenge, charged her to deny it, and briefly she looked at him again, her pulse fluttering agitatedly. 'It would certainly make things easier with three of you to distinguish,' she said, and for a moment his wide, firm mouth curved and softened into a smile.

'Grazie, signorina!'

His voice, pitched more deeply than normal, reminded her of the last time she had noticed that same deep, soft timbre. When it had whispered against her mouth only seconds before another woman's laughter broke the spell of an intimate moment, and she felt herself shiver at the memories it invoked.

'So!' Signor Cantorini conveyed a world of satisfaction with that one word, and his dark eyes smiled at her as he used his thin expressive hands to lend stress to his words. 'While Gianni is finding the book for Maria, Carlo, why do you not show Signorina Ramson some of the things she is here to see?'

'Volontàtiere!' From the way he got to his feet so quickly it might almost have indeed been true that he did so willingly, and he stood for a second looking down at Sara while she hesitated to comply with the old man's suggestion. 'Sara?'

The softly spoken use of her name, so gently inquiring, was irresistible, and she got to her feet, standing beside old Giovánni Cantorini for a second while she tried to bring her responsive senses under control. 'If you'll excuse me, Signor Cantorini.'

'Naturalmente, signorina! I am sure that you are anxious to see some of our beautiful things and Carlo will be delighted to show them to you. I wish that it

could have been my pleasant task, but——' Bony shoulders shrugged regretfully, and he spread his expressive hands. 'Carlo is a little less knowledgeable than I am, but infinitely more so than Gianni!'

His bright dark eyes glittered with mischievous amusement and belied the seriousness of his boast, as he used his hands to make extravagant gestures towards the door, almost as if he was anxious that they should be away before Gianni came back. Carlo stood with one large hand outspread, inviting her to come with him, and she smiled and nodded at the old man, then obeyed the invitation.

Little was said as they walked downstairs into that vast and beautiful hall that had so impressed her when she arrived with Gianni, but she was finding it dismayingly hard to give her attention to the beauties she was meant to be admiring when her senses were so urgently aware of the man beside her. Gianni was very good-looking and very attractive, but she would have been better able to appreciate her surroundings in his company.

'You like Titian?'

The inquiry, accompanied by a light finger-tip touch on her arm, snatched her back to reality and she looked instinctively at the painting that hung almost immediately facing her, lit by its own strip light. It showed an exquisitely lovely young woman with fair skin and soft, shy eyes, half smiling as she looked down from an ornate gilt frame. The work was unmistakable, as the wonderful harmony of colours were that formed the background to the portrait, and the folds of the sitter's formal dress.

Sara gazed at it for several seconds before she spoke, aware as she did so that she was herself under scrutiny by Carlo's dark, shadowed eyes. 'It's beautiful,' she breathed after a while. 'It's quite exquisitely beautiful.'

'And genuine, you think, Sara?'

'But of course it's genuine!' She turned swiftly from the portrait, her face flushed with the same hasty defensiveness that showed in her grey eyes. 'I wish you wouldn't be so sure that I'm here simply to discover more reproductions among your antiquities, Signor Cantorini! You're doing me an injustice if you think I came here only for that, or that I see these beautiful things merely as—as so much merchandise!'

It seemed so important to convince him and her anxiety to do so showed in the wide brightness of her eyes as she looked up at him. Why his opinion should matter so much was inexplicable at the moment, for he was almost a complete stranger to her, and yet it did, and the fact was in itself disturbing.

It was so quiet in the great hall, and his voice was pitched low, giving a suggestion of intimacy to his words. 'Must I then apologise yet again, Sara? It seems I am destined to do little else whenever we meet.'

Sara shook back her hair, trying to keep her own gaze steady in the face of those unnerving dark eyes as they scanned her flushed face. 'I don't want you to apologise, *signore*, just give me the benefit of the doubt once in a while, that's all!'

Briefly he looked up at the portrait then back again to Sara, and there was a warmth in his eyes that did strange and inexplicable things to her senses when she saw it there. 'Titian would have done justice to your grey eyes, Sara. Had you lived five hundred years ago you might now be smiling down at me from that portrait instead of frowning at me so angrily.'

Startled by the response he aroused in her, Sara hastily

looked away, seeking a distraction; and looking once more at the smooth painted face with its benign half-smile, she wondered if such submissive gentleness as the painting conveyed really would have appealed to him. One fact she took note of was that he had not made the same mistake Gianni had regarding the colour of her eyes.

'I'm not angry, Signor Cantorini——'

'Carlo!'

She flicked him a brief and half-defiant glance from the shadow of her lashes and did not reply. Instead she picked up a curious little figure of a Chinese man that stood immediately below the Titian, on a small table. It was white, delicately translucent and with the draping of the robes and the physical features of the face and body produced in remarkable detail.

'Blanc-de-Chine.' Her voice was much more unsteady than she anticipated as she turned the figure over in her hands. 'It's very beautiful.'

With one hand resting on the wall beside him, Carlo leaned slightly towards her, bringing the tinglingly evocative scent of after-shave mingled with the warmth of his body, and there was a gleam in his eyes that matched the sardonic smile on his mouth as he looked down at her.

'Our opinions of beauty appear to differ, *mia cara* Sara. You are right, of course, it is Blanc-de-Chine, but I would describe him as remarkable, incredible even, but never beautiful.'

'Oh, Carlo, stop it!' Her reaction surprised him, and she felt herself colour furiously as he looked down at her for a moment without speaking. Then before he had time to say anything, she hurried on, her voice breathless and slightly husky. 'You seem determined to make me angry, and I can't imagine why!'

'Perhaps because you look so lovely when you are angry.'

The sound of that deep, slow voice slid along her back like a sliver of ice, and she shivered. Holding her hands tightly together, she glanced back up the staircase they had just descended and licked her dry lips anxiously. She wasn't a young girl like the one he had brought to distract Gianni, and yet he could somehow make her feel as if she was.

'I think I'll wait until Gianni comes back, *signore*, if you don't mind. He promised to show me round and——'

'Gianni will be longer than you anticipate, *mia cara* Sara.' His dark eyes mocked her as he leaned once more against the wall and looked down at her with that sardonic smile on his mouth. 'He and Maria Laurana are——' His large expressive hands made signs in the air that were impossible to misinterpret, and Sara felt a small curl of embarrassment in her stomach. 'You understand?'

'Perfectly, *signore*!'

She held her handbag tightly in both hands, her eyes momentarily downcast while she summoned her courage, but all her efforts at self-control were undermined a second later when Carlo reached out with one hand and curved his long fingers about her cheek as he turned her head towards him.

'You do not take him seriously, Sara, eh? You have told me so.'

'No, I don't, but——'

'So you do not mind that he is with Maria Laurana?'

Sara shook her head. She felt quite alarmingly vulnerable suddenly and wished she had obeyed her initial instinct not to pay this visit to the villa. Now that Gianni had deserted her in favour of Maria Laurana, however reluctantly, she felt oddly superfluous, and she did not like the experience.

'Perhaps I should go,' she ventured. 'Another day might be more convenient. Gianni's preoccupied and I don't like to impose on you, Signor Cantorini.'

'Why are you so stubborn about using my name, Sara?' His fingers were curved once more about her cheek and he turned her face to him. 'Is it so distasteful to you?'

'Oh no, of course not!'

Yet again she was touched by the memory of his arms about her as they stood in the shadows of Ruga Parco, and her senses responded to his dark, sensual nearness with alarming urgency. She had never before been so physically aware of a man as she was of Carlo Cantorini and she found it difficult to believe that he could affect her the way he did.

'Come with me.'

The soft-voiced invitation startled her for a second, but she obeyed it automatically, and allowed him to lead her to one of the numerous rooms that led off the hall. It was large and ornate, just as the hall was and the room upstairs, but she was less conscious of her surroundings at the moment than she was of her companion, and Carlo Cantorini was smiling.

'There are many things you wish to see while you are here. It is why you came, is it not?'

Sara nodded, though she was not at all sure that it was quite all the truth. If she was honest, the thought of

100

Carlo Cantorini had been as much responsible for her final decision to come as the desire to see the beautiful things he had in his home. Briefly she thought she heard someone in the hall, and she glanced back over her shoulder, but made no move to discover whether or not it might be Gianni.

'You recognise Bellini and Canaletto?' Carlo's voice drew her attention to the masterpieces that hung on the walls, and she nodded recognition of them, but her mind was still on more personal matters.

'Is Gianni—serious about Signorina Laurana?'

Her question took him by surprise, she thought, but he was only a moment recovering, then he looked at her curiously as he shrugged his broad shoulders. 'It is hoped that he will become so in time. It would please both families.'

'Oh, I see.'

She was sure she did, Sara thought. A suitable alliance between two wealthy families was desirable, though probably there would be little regard paid to the feelings of the two people most involved. Possibly it would make very little difference to Gianni's life style, just as long as he was safely and respectably married.

She thought she could see more clearly now why his father was anxious not to have him become too involved with her. And why he had taken her to dinner himself, rather than risk Gianni breaking his earlier date with Maria Laurana to take her. It was something she found surprisingly bitter to swallow, but a distinct possibility she was forced to recognise.

'You do not approve?'

He looked down at her with that now almost familiar hint of challenge, and Sara did not quite know how to answer him. She was certain Gianni was not the type to be coerced into doing anything he strongly objected to, but she resented being regarded by his family as an undesirable distraction.

'It isn't really my concern,' she told him in a small and distinctly uncertain voice. 'As I'm sure you'll agree, *signore*.' She looked up at him with the resentment showing clearly in her grey eyes. 'That's the reason you're taking the trouble to show me around yourself, isn't it? So that Gianni won't be distracted. And why you took me out to dinner, so that you'd be quite sure he didn't come for me after all?'

'You little fool!'

His vehemence startled her, but before she could recover sufficiently to object to his opinion, he pulled her to him, his hands pressing her close; so close she could feel the passion that burned in him, like fire in her own body. His mouth parted her lips with bruising urgency, and for a few delirious moments she yielded to her own wanton instincts.

It was only the persistent nagging reminder in her brain that he sought only to offer a distraction from Gianni that brought her to her senses. She turned her face from the clinging fierceness of his mouth, her hands pushing at the almost unbreakable strength of his arms, and stepped back from him, her breathing rapid and uneven.

She scarcely recognised her own voice in the light, breathless whisper that issued from her lips, and her honey-fair hair swung forward to hide her flushed cheeks while she rejected the clamouring excitement that raced through her body after the last few minutes.

'You have no need to worry, *signore*, I won't spoil your

plans for Gianni, though I wouldn't be too certain of them if your son is as ruthless as you are in the pursuit of his own way!' She clenched her hands tightly to stop them trembling and lifted her chin, meeting his eyes for a second only before hastily turning away. 'Please give my apologies to Signor Cantorini, and explain that I couldn't stay for lunch after all. *Addio, signore!'*

CHAPTER SIX

It was getting near to lunch time, but Sara had not even noticed the time. Ever since her hurried and rather emotional parting from Carlo Cantorini four days ago, she had busied herself more industriously than ever around the shop, hoping that by doing so she would not have to dwell on the reason for her hasty departure. No matter how often she told herself that Carlo Cantorini was a stranger whom she scarcely knew, remembering the excitement of being in his arms could disturb her all too easily, and she was trying her hardest to forget what happened.

She vowed that if Gianni ever came to see her again, she would send him away with a reminder that Maria Laurana was a much more suitable companion for him. She would do nothing that would allow Carlo to think she was encouraging his son.

Cris had found her manner rather puzzling the past few days. Not that he had said anything to her, but his dark eyes watched her curiously whenever he thought himself unnoticed, and she had interrupted a conversation with his mother only last night, that she was pretty sure concerned herself, because it ceased abruptly when she joined them.

The jangling summons of the door bells jolted her out of her day-dream, and she looked up and smiled automatically at the two men who came in. *'Buon giorno, signori.'*

'Buon giorno, Signorina Ramson!'

It was only when he spoke that Sara recognised the older of two men as Gianni's great-grandfather, old Giovanni Cantorini, and her pulse leapt alarmingly as she tried to speculate on just why he was there. He was interested in antiques, or course, but somehow she did not believe that he was there to see her in her professional capacity, no matter how flattering he had been about her ability.

Remembering how abruptly she had left his home, without seeing him or making an explanation to him personally, she coloured furiously. 'Signor Cantorini— *buon giorno, signore*.'

Her voice had an oddly breathless sound, and she could sense Cris, standing beside her, taking more than a cursory interest now that he knew the identity of the caller. She did not know what to say, and she swallowed hard as she tried to summon some kind of apology without betraying the reason for her lack of good manners at their last meeting.

'Signor Cantorini, I—I have to apologise to you. I mean, I shouldn't have behaved as I did, and I hope you'll accept my word that I acted on impulse, and——'

'I am aware of your reason for departing so hastily, *mia cara signorina*, please do not upset yourself.'

'Thank you.'

She still hesitated to look at him as directly as she would normally have done, especially now that she knew he was aware of why she had left the villa so hurriedly. He probably thought her incredibly naïve for reacting the way she had, particularly since his son was well known as having a taste for a variety of women-friends. He would see nothing untoward in his behaviour.

She could feel Cris's curious dark eyes flicking between

her and her unexpected caller, trying to understand what was going on. The old man walked proudly upright, even though he used a stick for support, and the man with him was apparently a servant, hovering close by in case he was needed. What the reason was for his visit, she still could not decide, and she felt strangely apprehensive as he made his way towards her.

But tall and autocratic as he appeared, the dark, hawk-like face was smiling when he removed an old-fashioned, wide brimmed straw hat and held it against his chest while he spoke. 'If you wish to make amends for your hasty departure, *signorina*, the means are at your disposal.'

Uncertainly Sara blinked and shook her head. 'Of course, *signore*, if I can.'

'I was passing your premises, *signorina*, and the temptation to invite you to lunch was irresistible. You will not refuse me, eh?'

Taken completely off guard, Sara wavered. 'Oh! Well —Signor Cantorini, I——'

'Ah, come, *signorina*, why should you refuse me, huh?' She was given no more time to decide whether or not she wished to accept, the decision was taken for her. Turning to Cris, he spoke sharply and authoritatively in a way that brooked no argument, '*La borsa della* Signorina Ramson, *ragazzo. Fretta, fretta!*'

'*Si, signore!*'

Cris did not hesitate but hurried as he was told and fetched Sara's handbag for her. Obviously he was impressed with such autocracy, and he jumped to obey with equal alacrity when the old man spoke again. '*La chiave, ragazzo, la chiave!* The premises cannot be left unlocked while the *signorina* is absent!'

Having reached down the key of the shop Cris hesitated before giving it to Sara, probably wondering if he should hand it instead to the old man who had issued the order. Dazed by the speed of events, Sara took it absently, her fingers stiff and uncertain.

'Signor Cantorini, I really can't just close up the shop like this.'

'*Assurdità!*'

A bony and imperious hand dismissed her doubts, and she found herself already on the way to the door with Signor Cantorini's hand holding tightly to her arm, while Cris and the manservant followed close behind. Once outside Cris took the key from her and locked the door, looking at her inquiringly when he handed it back, and Sara looked at him somewhat vaguely as she shook her head.

'You'd—you'd better go and have lunch, Cris; I'll see you later.'

'*Si, signorina.*' Cris, as always her self-appointed bodyguard, was obviously in two minds about leaving her, and he hovered for a moment, trying to summon enough courage to outface the aged autocrat who seemed to have laid claim to her. 'You will be—O.K., *signorina*?'

'Oh yes, Cris, I'll be O.K., thank you.' His concern for her was touching and she smiled at him, albeit a little dazedly, for she was still far from sure just what Giovanni Cantorini had in mind for her. 'You go and have your lunch, I'll see you later.'

'*Si, signorina.*'

He turned off across the *campo* in the direction of their usual lunchtime rendezvous, and Signor Cantorini smiled after his departing figure approvingly. 'You have many admirers, I think, *mia cara signorina*, eh?'

'Cris is very—concerned for me. He's a very charming boy.'

The old man's eyes twinkled at her from his hawkish face as he turned her in the opposite direction from that Cris had taken, his fingers holding tightly to her arm. 'A boy to you, perhaps, Signorina Ramson, but in Italy he is a young man already, and with an eye for a *bella signorina*, eh?'

Sara remembered Cris's eagerness to see his convent schoolgirl each evening, and thought he could perhaps be more mature than she had so far realised. At the moment, however, her own situation took precedence over Cris's. Maybe she should have taken a firmer stand over being told to close up the shop and accompany this autocratic old man to lunch.

Old Giovanni Cantorini was much more active than she could have expected. Heaven knew where he was taking her, but he was determined, and from what little experience she had so far had of the men of the Cantorini family, she thought there would have been little use in offering resistance.

The thin hand on her arm impelled rather than led, and his step was firm and confident, even though a little stiff; the manservant walking half a pace in the rear instead of lending his arm for support. Presumably they had come from the Villa Cantorini by motor launch, but at the moment they continued on foot, and the old man showed no sign of flagging.

They turned along a narrow *calle* almost at once, and that in turn led to another *campo*, very similar to the one they had just left, one that Sara had had no idea existed until now, even though it was close to where she worked. It was simply part of the intriguing maze that was Venice.

A few more steps brought them to what must once have been a delightful Renaissance villa. Facing on to the square, its elegant façade showed the same slightly rakish air of outward neglect that characterised the Villa Cantorini, and was in some curious way part of their charm.

It was smaller than the *palazzo* where Carlo had taken her, but converted to the same purpose, and reminiscent of it in many ways. It appeared equally luxurious inside, which probably explained why Cris had taken her instead to the smaller and less expensive *osteria* they normally frequented, even though it was not as near to the shop.

A few tables overflowed into the square itself, but most of the accommodation was inside—small tables for the most part, set with snow-white linen and good silver, the limited space given an illusion of greater size by long gilded wall mirrors that reflected the elegant room from every angle.

Her host was evidently known, for he was greeted with smiles and an air that amounted almost to reverence, all of which he seemingly took for granted, though with a certain graciousness that characterised all his dealings with others. They were shown to a table with an excellent view of the little square, and away from the worst of the heat, while the manservant remained outside at one of the exterior tables, on hand but unobtrusive.

Two waiters attended them, one seeing the old man seated while the other still hovered behind Sara's chair, waiting for her to take her seat. Instead she took her first decisive and definite action since they left the shop, and stood looking across at her host, smiling but decided.

'If you'll excuse me for a moment, Signor Cantorini.'

He looked across at her inquiringly, as if he half suspected she might be going to have second thoughts about lunching with him after all. *'Signorina?'*

'I really must make myself a little more presentable before I have lunch,' she explained, and shook her head as she smiled. 'I didn't even have time to wash my hands.'

'Ah, *mia cara signorina*, forgive me!' The dark eyes twinkled at her, faintly malicious in the way she had seen Gianni's look. 'I did not wish to give you the opportunity to refuse me, but I trust you not to run away from *me*, eh?'

The reference to her hasty departure from Carlo and the Villa Cantorini brought a flush to her cheeks, and she shook her head. 'I'll be back, *signore*. I need just a few minutes to freshen up.'

'Si, certamente, signorina!'

Sara left him seated at the small table, and smiled to herself as she went into the ladies' room. Heaven knew what his motive was in asking her to lunch with him, but he had that autocratic but irresistible charm that typified the Cantorini men, and she was nothing loth to share a meal with him.

A few minutes was all she needed to wash and renew what little make-up she wore, and she emerged from the cloakroom feeling much better able to cope with whatever came along next. She was no more than halfway back to their table when she saw and recognised a tall, lean figure standing with its back to her, and talking to her host.

She had been prepared for almost anything, but not

for finding Carlo there, and she thought she saw at last why old Giovanni Cantorini had issued that unexpected invitation to lunch. It would explain his anxious, hustling refusal to take no for an answer, though why he was so keen for her and Carlo to meet again after their last disastrous encounter, she could not imagine.

Carlo still had his back to her, and she thanked heaven for it at the moment, for she felt dismayingly unsteady as she made her way back to the table on legs that trembled as if they would not much longer support her. He was wearing a fawn suit with a brown silk shirt, and he looked as darkly and sternly attractive as the last time she had seen him.

When she got within hearing distance she realised he was saying something to his grandfather; asking him something, judging by the tone of his voice. He spoke in Italian, but seeing Sara coming up behind him, Signor Cantorini made his reply in English.

'I am lunching with a friend, Carlo, but you are most welcome to join us, if you wish.'

There was a long mirror on the wall behind the old man and in it Sara could see Carlo's face. She detected the fleeting glimpse of perplexity in his dark eyes caused by the strange tongue and then he too glanced into the mirror and saw her almost immediately behind him. He hesitated, then turned swiftly, his dark gaze noting her flushed face and the sudden evasiveness of her eyes.

'Signorina.'

He was so coolly distant that for a moment Sara's heart lurched anxiously. 'Signore?'

'You will join us, Carlo, si?'

The old man was pressing, confident of his reply, but Sara feared he was going to refuse the invitation and simply walk off. It seemed like an eternity before he inclined his head in a brief, abrupt acknowledgment of acceptance, then drew out her chair for her, his hard fingers brushing her arm for a second, and bringing an urgent flutter of reaction from her pulse.

The smallness of the tables precluded any possibility of being distant from the others seated at the same table, and she was immediately aware of that disturbing sense of excitement that Carlo Cantorini could arouse in her, even here, in a public restaurant. The unmistakable twinkle in the old man's eyes made it even more certain that he had anticipated this meeting, and she found it even harder to remain cool and collected when she thought of Carlo being just as aware of it.

She gazed at the menu in her hand uncomprehendingly, trying to still the frantic response of her senses, and unable to understand any of what she read. The last time she had eaten a meal with Carlo, she had left the choice to him, and this time she was in even more need of assistance with the incomprehensible Italian.

Appealing to her host, she smiled apologetically. 'Signor Cantorini, I wonder if you'd help me, please.' She laughed a little shakily and shook her head. 'I don't know what to order, I don't read Italian, and——'

'*Naturalmente, naturalmente!*' The old man inclined his head in the direction of his grandson. 'Alas, I cannot assist you myself, *mia cara signorina*, I do not have my spectacles with me, but I am sure that Carlo will help you to choose. Will you not, Carlo?'

'Of course.' He leaned towards her, holding the double-paged menu for her inspection, and the move brought him so close that once more that heady combination of after-shave and masculine warmth teased her senses. 'Do you have any special preference, *signorina*?'

'I—I'll have to rely on you, I'm afraid,' she told him, coping with the renewed urgency of her heartbeat. 'Will you please choose something for me?'

'*Certamente!*'

He scanned the list briefly, then chose various items from it, consulting her on each item in his soft, deep voice before confirming it with the waiter, and she nodded agreement without even considering. It was only when she began to eat that she realised just how much she had to get through.

The clear, rich soup he ordered for her was excellent, and she was enjoying a *fritto misto* of fish with a green salad when their host announced his decision to leave them. He had ordered only one course; a substantial *minestrone* it was true, but a much lighter meal than either of his guests, pleading old age as the reason for his lack of appetite. The soup finished, he called in his manservant from outside and smiled apologetically at Sara.

'I regret that I cannot share the rest of your meal, *mia cara signorina*, but——' Expressive shoulders both excused and apologised as he got to his feet.

Sara looked up at him uncertainly, her heart beating hard and fast when she realised just how obvious the move must look to his grandson. Her own reactions were so confused that she made no attempt to decide whether she was dismayed or delighted at being left alone with Carlo; some response she felt was called for.

'Signor Cantorini, must you go? I mean,' she added hastily, 'it seems such a pity that you've eaten so little.'

'Do not let my lack of appetite discourage you, *per favore*. I grow tired too easily these days and I cannot be as active as I would wish, *signorina*. Enjoy your luncheon and each other's company, eh?'

Sara carefully avoided looking at Carlo. He was on his feet, waiting patiently for his grandfather to leave before resuming his meal and apparently less concerned than Sara that he had eaten so little. The old man took her hand, lifting her fingers to his lips and smiling in a way that made nonsense of his claim to weariness.

'I shall hope to see you again at the Villa Cantorini before very long, *mia cara signorina*, and next time you will not run away before we have given you lunch, eh?' His chuckle brought a quick flush to her cheeks as he turned away, using his stick but declining the arm of his man as he walked straight and proud through the restaurant. '*Arrivederci, signorina!*'

Sara watched him as far as the street before she resumed her meal, his step only slightly slow; replacing the old-fashioned straw hat on his white head when he stepped out into the sunshine outside. He was a remarkable old man, but quite as accustomed to getting what he wanted as his grandson and great-grandson were, and she wished in this case she knew exactly what it was he did want.

Quite clearly Carlo had recognised his grandfather's tactics as easily as Sara had, but he solemnly stood while the old man left their table, sitting down again only when he was out of sight. He was pouring more wine into Sara's glass when he caught her eye, and the glint of laughter she saw there took her so by surprise that she felt her pulse leap wildly in response to it.

One black brow flicked upward and he leaned his elbows on the table in front of him as he took another sip of wine, looking at her steadily from below half lowered lids. 'I hope you are not embarrassed by my grandfather's obvious matchmaking, Sara?'

The dark strong face became softer and younger somehow when he smiled, and Sara found it incredibly difficult to control the sudden urgency of her heartbeat. More than ever aware of that mingling of masculine scents, and the long brown hands that held his wine glass, she looked down at her own glass rather than at him, and her smile was much less confident.

'But surely Signor Cantorini wouldn't be—matchmaking. I mean, surely you don't think——'

'Oh, but I *do*!' He was apparently in no doubt at all, yet he seemingly saw less reason to be embarrassed about it than she did herself. Instead he seemed to be finding it rather amusing. 'Does it make you angry, Sara?'

The way he pronounced her name made it sound quite different to its English sound, and much prettier, and she wished he did not have the effect he did on her senses. He should have resented his grandfather's deviousness in planning this lunch with the specific intention of leaving them alone together, and she could not understand him at all.

'It might make me angry if I thought it was serious.' She chose her words carefully, realising how easily she could sound offensive. 'In fact,' she confessed, looking at him through her lashes, 'I thought *you'd* be annoyed.'

'Did you?' He spoke quietly, and the timbre of his voice was like a velvet finger along her spine. Leaning forward, he rested his elbows on the table once more, his glass held in both hands with its rim pressed to his lips while he regarded her steadily. 'Why, Sara?'

'I—I don't know exactly.' She had seen him as a man

who would resent any kind of interference in his private life, and she felt he *should* be resenting it—she could not imagine why he wasn't. 'Unless—perhaps you're used to Signor Cantorini——'

'Trying to marry me off? Is that not your expression?' His dark eyes glittered, though whether or not with amusement she could not determine. She only knew that she was finding this conversation increasingly embarrassing. 'Does the idea embarrass you, Sara?' His wide mouth curved into a sardonic smile as he twirled his glass between long brown fingers. 'You should not let it—Nonno would like to see me married again, but he has never gone to quite such lengths before I am forced to admit!'

'Oh, but I can't believe he was serious!' Her voice sounded curiously breathless suddenly. 'Not where I am concerned, he couldn't be, I'm sure——'

'Oh, but I am sure he was, Sara.' The deep quiet voice was so confident that Sara's heart gave a breathtaking lurch in her breast and she shook her head slowly but insistently. 'Nonno has what you call a soft spot for you, huh?'

It was difficult to believe this conversation was taking place, harder still to believe that Carlo Cantorini was taking it all so matter-of-factly. She felt suddenly as if she had got into much deeper water than she could safely cope with. The whole episode had become far more intimate and personal than she wanted, and there seemed little she could do to check it.

'I—I hardly think that's likely,' she denied in a small and rather breathless voice. 'Signor Cantorini hardly knows me and—well, I'm not even Italian.'

'Nor was Gianni's mother.'

It couldn't be happening, Sara thought wildly, it just could not be happening. He was talking as if he took it all quite seriously and that simply wasn't possible. She had vowed not to let herself become too involved with the Cantorinis, and yet it seemed to be increasingly difficult to remain aloof from them.

'Gianni told me his mother was English.' She chanced a brief upward glance and laughed unsteadily, hoping she sounded no more than politely interested. 'It accounts for those hazel eyes, of course—it's the only un-Italian thing about him!'

She was aware that Carlo was watching her still instead of concentrating on his meal. 'Do you dislike Italians, Sara?'

That deep, quiet voice slid along her spine in its shivering softness and she laughed, picking up her wine glass and looking into it as she spoke rather than directly at him. 'Good heavens, no! It isn't possible to make a sweeping statement like that about any race, surely, is it?'

'Perhaps not.' He made the concession absently, still watching her from across the small table, his dark eyes level and unwavering. 'But you admire Nonno, do you not, Sara?'

She smiled, willing enough to commit herself on that point. Giovanni Cantorini might be autocratic and, as she had discovered today, devious, but she liked him. He had the same unfailing charm that his grandson and his great-grandson had, and she had to admit to finding it irresistible, however unwise she might be.

'I like him very much indeed,' she conceded without hesitation. 'I think he's charming and gallant, and quite remarkable for his age.'

Carlo's eyes glittered, one black brow flicking upward. 'Perhaps,' he suggested, soft-voiced, 'we should match you with Nonno!'

Laughter brought mobility and an unexpected gentleness to the stern features, and she tried to control the suddenly urgent beat of her heart. It was incredible how he could stir such responses in her, and she despaired of ever remaining as aloof as she had vowed to, where Carlo was concerned.

'Carlo——'

She got no further, for he reached across and lightly touched her cheek, and instinctively she closed her eyes for a second. His dark eyes watched her, steady and inquiring, his meal apparently forgotten. 'But you would not like to disappoint him completely, eh, *mia cara* Sara?' Looking up swiftly, she saw again the bright glint of laughter in his eyes. 'Will you come out with me this evening? Dinner, perhaps?'

It had not even crossed his mind that she might refuse, Sara guessed as she coped with a rapid heartbeat that left her breathless and lent a husky, tremulous sound to her voice. And she had never felt more disappointed in her life that she had to refuse—she had no option.

'I'm sorry, Carlo.' His frown was swift and dark, and she hastened to enlighten him as to her reasons for refusing. 'I've no alternative, you see. I've been so—so miserable these past few days that Signora Vincenti has arranged for a few friends to come in this evening. A kind of cheering up party, I suppose you'd call it.'

'Ah!' The speculative gleam in his eyes puzzled her for a moment. 'You have been unhappy for the past few days?' She shrugged uneasily, realising that by telling him that she had also told him the reason for her unhappiness. 'Since you ran away from me on Sunday, eh, Sara?'

'I felt rather ashamed.' She sought to supply an excuse that did not make her unhappiness personal to him, although she was fairly sure he would not believe it. 'I shouldn't have left as I did without saying a word to Signor Cantorini. I'm only surprised he took the trouble to come and see me, after the way I behaved.'

'Have I not said that he has a soft spot for you?' She smiled and shook her head, though she realised now that it was probably true to a degree. 'Tomorrow I cannot see you, I have someone much less charming and attractive to see on a matter of business, but you will be free all day on Sunday, will you not, Sara? Will you spend it with me?'

Her heart was beating rapidly and her whole body felt as if she was about to shiver violently in response to that deep, soft voice trying to persuade her. She had no need to be persuaded, she was already thinking of Sunday, and the thought of spending a whole day in his company. A slight flush in her cheeks gave her a bright glow that was reflected in her grey eyes, as shiny as jewels.

'I'd like to, Carlo.'

One large brown hand reached across the small table and touched her fingers, enclosing them lightly at first and then more firmly, until she felt the warm strength of him impressed on her soft flesh. '*Bene,*' he said softly. 'And this time you will not run away from me, *no?*'

His laughter teased her, but something in the dark, luminous eyes sent a shivering thrill through her body. 'I won't run away,' she promised.

Not for the first time Sara felt rather guilty because she was not fully appreciating Signora Vincenti's efforts on her behalf. It was not exactly a party, but several people had been invited for the evening for wine and a buffet meal, and in other circumstances Sara would have appreciated their company, but tonight she kept remembering that she could have spent the evening with Carlo instead.

She had put on a pretty yellow dress that emphasised the curving softness of her figure, and her hair was brushed until its honey-gold shone like silk, but the glow in her eyes came from remembering the strength of Carlo's hand enclosing hers, and the promise of a whole day spent in his company. Maybe it would not be as exciting as she anticipated, but she found it hard not to believe it would.

She had mingled well with the guests, and one or two of them showed a definite interest in the fact that her uncle had married Signora Vincenti's sister. A popular question seemed to be whether or not Sara herself was likely to follow in her uncle's footsteps and marry an Italian. The interest was genuine and kindly meant, but in the circumstances she found it embarrassing, though she did her best to conceal the fact.

There was wine in plenty and an amazingly varied selection of buffet dishes, for Signora Vincenti did not often have the opportunity to play hostess, and she made the most of her chance when it occurred. Her husband was not a home-loving man, which was unusual for an Italian, but he was charming and polite to everyone, not least to Sara, whom he very obviously admired. She did her best not to let him corner her for too long, but he was confident of his way with women, and once or twice he had managed to get her to himself.

It was fairly late in the evening when she slipped out into the balcony garden for some fresh air, and sat for a while looking out across the canal where it twinkled with a myriad lights and reflections, thinking about Carlo Cantorini once more as she had done for most of the evening.

A footfall behind her made her swing round quickly, suspecting that her host had discovered her yet again and prepared to repulse him much more firmly this time. But it wasn't Signor Vincenti, it was Cris, and she smiled instead and sat back on the arm of one of the garden chairs.

Seeing him she was reminded that Giovanni Cantorini had said she should not regard him as a boy, but a young man, and looking at him in the artificial light that cast shadows and deepened lines, she was prepared to agree. Cris was only a month or two off his seventeenth birthday and he looked a young man, rather than a boy—a very good-looking young man with thoughtful dark eyes.

Sitting on another chair arm, he regarded her for a moment in silence. 'You are very—quiet, Sara. Is it that you do not enjoy your party after all?'

'But of course I'm enjoying it!' She would not have him believe anything else, after all the trouble his mother had gone to. 'I'm just taking a breather, that's all.'

Cris drank wine, as most Italian youngsters did, and he took a slow sip from his glass before he said anything else. 'You look across the water as if you are thinking of—someone.' He studied the wine in his glass for a second, thoughtfully, and it crossed her mind that he had had just a little too much of it already. 'Of Signor Carlo Cantorini, perhaps?'

'What makes you say that?'

Taken by surprise, she needed a moment to come to terms with the fact, and Cris shrugged his eloquent shoulders. 'I saw you leave *il signore* when I returned to the shop, Sara, and you have the—look of absence since then. Tonight you think of other things than our guests!'

At the moment Sara saw no reason to deny it. She had thought of nothing else but Carlo all evening, and there was no reason to deny the fact. Nevertheless her smile was a little uneasy. 'You're very astute, Cris.' She laughed, turning back to study the lights on the other side of the canal. 'I'm spending the day with Carlo on Sunday.'

'Ah!' Whatever that was meant to convey, he evidently understood perfectly how she was feeling, and once more his mature outlook surprised her. 'It is hard to always think of one special one, eh, Sara? It makes the mind absent.'

His own mood was different too, she realised, and looked at him curiously. 'You're being very profound, Cris. What's on *your* mind?'

'A young lady.' He made the statement with such quiet confidence that she blinked at him for a moment uncertainly. Bunching the fingers of one hand, he kissed their tips, closing his eyes as he did so. '*Molto bella!* I am in love, Sara!'

'Cris!' Briefly her own situation was forgotten when she recalled Cris's eagerness to see his convent girl. She had even let him go off one evening so that he could see her, and at the moment that thought made her curiously uneasy, though she wasn't sure why. 'You can't be serious, surely?'

'*Naturalmente!* My Maria, she is—oh, *molto bella*—so beautiful!'

Sara looked at him uneasily. 'Cris, it isn't your—the girl at the convent school, is it?'

Dark eyes glowing, Cris nodded eagerly. '*Si, si!* But she is not a schoolgirl, Sara, she is seventeen years and a woman! I love her so much I think I will die of love!'

He was quite serious, Sara realised, and wondered what on earth she should say. It was doubtful if either Cris's parents or the girl's realised what was going on, and she wondered if the girl herself had any idea or if Cris was simply nursing an unrequited passion. 'Cris, you haven't——'

'We have spoken, no more,' he hastened to assure her, his dark eyes reproaching her for harbouring less charitable thoughts. As he gazed out across the water there was a bright, dreamy look in his eyes. 'She is *bellissima*, Sara!'

Still uneasy about her own part in encouraging it, however briefly, Sara smiled anxiously. 'I'm sure she is, Cris, but you're taking an awful chance, aren't you?' She shrugged when he turned and looked at her. 'I mean, if her parents found out——'

'Hah!' Cris dismissed them with a scornful hand, his eyes blazing with defiance. 'They would marry her to a man of their choosing. What do they know of her heart?' He struck his own chest dramatically. 'Maria loves me, as I do her with all my heart, and if they do not agree, then we will go away together—it is planned!'

'Oh, Cris, no!'

'We shall make plans,' he insisted, but his sudden

change of tense registered immediately with Sara, and she breathed a little more easily.

'You mean you haven't really—not actually planned to run away?'

'Not yet.' Cris admitted it reluctantly, it was clear, and she took heart from the fact. 'But we are much in love, Sara.'

'Yes, I'm sure you are.'

He was looking at her, his good-looking young face much less mature suddenly, his dark eyes deep and soulful, earnest in their appeal. 'You will keep my secret, Sara?'

It was irresistible, and she felt strangely close to Cris suddenly, as if they shared a similar experience. Yet there was no earthly reason to suppose that they did. Her own feelings for Carlo Cantorini were very mixed at the moment, and it was virtually certain that he was far from succumbing to his grandfather's attempts at matchmaking, no matter how matter-of-factly he had accepted them. He had invited her to spend a day with him, that was all, and she was probably no more than one more momentary distraction in his very busy life.

She placed an arm around Cris's shoulders and hugged him briefly, smiling at the dark Italian look of him with affection. 'Of course I won't tell anyone, Cris; you have my word on it, just as long as you don't do anything silly.'

'*Grazie!*'

He made no promise, but she was convinced in her heart, and that was enough. Those dark Italian looks she found unfailingly persuasive lately.

CHAPTER SEVEN

SARA wanted to look absolutely right, and she had spent a long time getting ready. The dress she wore was new; deep gold with a pattern of tiny light green leaves, it showed off her lightly tanned skin as well as the honey-gold of her hair, soft and feminine and just a little bolder than usual in the neckline.

She wished she could have acquired a deeper tan, but she spent so much time indoors, in the shop, that her time for sunbathing was limited, also her skin wasn't the type that turned really brown no matter how long it was exposed. Instead she had turned a light gold that went well with her hair and eyes.

There was a curious little fluttering sensation in her stomach that was accounted for by the mingled excitement and apprehension she felt. Apprehension because she feared it was all too likely that she was going to make a complete fool of herself and fall in love with Carlo Cantorini, and that was something she wished desperately to avoid.

It would probably have been much more sensible to turn down his invitation, but somehow she did not think she could have done it. The prospect of spending a whole day with him was the most exciting thing that had happened to her since she came to Venice, and she could only hope that she did not live to regret it.

Picking up her handbag from the bed, she turned from the mirror with a rueful grimace, and emerged from her room only to come face to face with Cris. His good-looking young face always expressed how he felt, and it showed instant appreciation when he saw her. Kissing the tips of his bunched fingers, he rolled his eyes heavenward in apparent ecstasy.

'*Molto bella*, Sara!' He eyed her with a frankness that she was only now beginning to accept without embarrassment. 'You will knock out the eyes, eh?'

'Do you think so?' She felt slightly lightheaded, and smoothed a hand down her skirt as she sought further reassurance. 'I hope it's the right sort of thing for wherever I'm going.'

'*E perfetto*, Sara, no matter where you go! I think so, and I am sure Signor Carlo Cantorini will think so too. He is the expert on such things, *si*?'

Cris, like his mother, still did not trust the Cantorini, and Carlo in particular, but Sara did not like to have his dislike made so obvious, not at the moment when she was much too unsure of herself. At any other time she would have tackled him with his frankness, but instead she let it pass for the moment, and glanced instead over her shoulder at the stairs.

It was impossible to hear the front door bell from her room, and she looked at Cris inquiringly when she recalled that she had found him right outside her door when she opened it. 'Is Signor Cantorini here yet, Cris?'

There was the slightest suggestion of a tremor in her voice, and Cris noticed it, looking at her curiously as he answered. '*Si*, he is here, I have just admitted him to the *entrata*, Sara.'

'Oh, then I'm keeping him waiting.'

Somehow she hadn't expected Carlo to be early and it gave her an added cause for excitement to think that he was already waiting for her downstairs. Cris, however, was shrugging off the possibility of Carlo Cantorini becoming impatient.

'He waits—but one does not complain when one is expecting a lovely woman, Sara.'

Such self-assurance would probably have amused her in other circumstances, but at the moment she did not feel able to share his casual approach. Smoothing down her skirt once more, she smiled at him. 'Just the same, I'd better go. Please say goodbye to your mother for me, will you, Cris? *Ciao!*'

'*Ciao, bella* Sara!' Cris beamed her one of his dazzling smiles. '*Buon divertimente!*'

It remained to be seen whether or not she enjoyed herself, but Sara's heart was fluttering anxiously as she hurried downstairs, and there was nothing she could do about the shaky unsteadiness of her legs. It was quite ridiculous to feel as she did—she was old enough to cope with someone like Carlo Cantorini without feeling like an excited schoolgirl going on a first date.

There were a couple of ancient armchairs in the hall, but Carlo had chosen to stand and wait for her. Standing back in the shadows he appeared as a vague dark figure at first, then he turned to look at her as she came down the stairs and the sudden whiteness of his teeth showed for a moment in the tanned face when he smiled.

He wore a beige suit that somehow made him look taller, and a dark shirt, open at the neck to show a strong brown throat, and Sara half closed her eyes on the inevitable effect he had on her senses. He was smoking, but he discarded the cigarette as soon as he saw her and came across on long, smooth strides to take her hand.

His fingers felt cool and hard, but he did not squeeze her hand as Gianni would have done. Instead he raised it to his lips after a second or two and lightly touched her fingers with his mouth, while his dark gaze swept slowly over her face. Her cheeks had a slight flush and there was a brightness in her grey eyes that gave them a jewel-like glow between shadowing lashes when she briefly looked up at him, then as hastily looked away.

'I was almost afraid that you would not come after all, Sara. I am so glad that I was wrong.'

Such a statement coming from Carlo was completely unexpected, and she showed her surprise quite clearly when she looked at him. 'You didn't think I'd come?' She could still hardly believe it.

From the way he shrugged his broad shoulders it seemed likely he regretted making the admission, and there was a slightly sardonic smile about that wide, expressive mouth as he shook his head. 'I am not very sure what I thought, *cara mia*.' Once again he scanned her face and smiled. 'Maybe I thought you would not come because you still do not completely trust me, *si*?'

'Oh no, you're wrong, I——'

'No, no, no!' She caught her breath when a firm finger was placed over her lips, easing after a second and pulling down her bottom lip before letting go. 'Do not deny it, Sara, *per favore*. One of the things I like about you is your honesty, and I would not have you disillusion me!'

It was so difficult to remain cool and in control when he stood so close, looking down at her with a shadow of a smile in his dark eyes. His voice too played havoc with her senses and it was going to be so much harder than she had anticipated, trying to keep a cool head when she was with him all day. Nevertheless she had to try.

'You do not completely trust me, do you, Sara?'

He asked the question so softly that she scarcely heard

it for the loud, thudding beat of her heart, and she was shaking her head rapidly to and fro almost without conscious effort.

'Of course I do, Carlo. I shouldn't be coming with you if I didn't.'

'No?'

It seemed he wanted yet more assurances, and this shadow of uncertainty in him was so unexpected that it gave her a new insight suddenly; made him so much more human. It was instinctive to reach out and touch him, but she held back, deterred as much by the violence of her own emotions as by any wariness of him.

'I wish you'd believe me,' she said, husky-voiced.

For a second or two he said nothing, but looked down into her face, his gaze as always unwavering, then once more that brief, sardonic hint of smile touched his mouth. '*Benissimo*—then I will!' A hand slid beneath her arm, strong fingers curling into her soft skin as he turned her towards the outside door and the sunlit street. 'Where would you like to go, Sara?'

Stepping so suddenly out into the sunshine after the dimness of the hall dazzled her for a moment and she shook her head as she fell into step beside him, his hand still guiding her along the narrow *calle*. 'I—I haven't really thought about it,' she confessed. 'I thought perhaps you might have some idea——'

'I have an idea.' He led her past the landing stage that was almost immediately below the Vincentis' balcony, so evidently he was on foot at the moment. 'I thought perhaps you would like to be the complete tourist and sail along *il Canale Grande* in a gondola, *si*? Does that appeal to you, Sara?'

'Oh, I'd love it!'

He pulled a face at her enthusiasm and there was a glow of mockery in his eyes, but for all that she felt he was pleased by her response and just for a moment the hand on her arm squeezed gently. '*Bene*, then that is what we will do!'

'You won't——' She hesitated to suggest that he was going to be utterly bored acting as her guide, but for the moment she had forgotten that no Venetian is ever bored with his city, or of showing it off to visitors. 'If you're sure you don't mind.'

'*Mia cara* Sara, do you think that I would suggest such a trip if I minded?'

'No.' She looked up at that strong, arrogant face and the challenging gleam in his eyes, and knew the question was reasonable enough coming from Carlo Cantorini. 'No—no, of course you wouldn't.'

The Grand Canal was unlike anything else in the world, and Sara took a devotee's view of it, ignoring the imperfections and seeing only the beauty and history that rose up on either side of her as they were propelled gently along on the water.

It was customary, so she had been led to believe, for the gondolier to sing out the names of the many places of interest along the route, but in her case she had no need of the services of the gondolier with Carlo to instruct her. The man merely guided their craft along, wielding his long pole with the skill of long practice.

She felt dazed with the names and histories of so many palaces and churches as they made their way through the crowd of other craft, their gondolier occasionally shouting imprecations at the faster *vaporetto* and *motoscàfo* drivers who came too close. Their passionate and uninhibited use of the human voice was, Sara felt, part of the Italian charm, and she enjoyed every second of it. Even their curses had a certain lyrical quality to the uninitiated ear.

It was virtually impossible to sit upright in the seating provided, and she was more or less obliged to relax against the cushions, encircled by the curve of Carlo's arm. It was not only instinctive but inevitable in the circumstances and he seemed to accept the situation as quite the natural thing to do.

Snuggled down beside him as she was, the tingling mixture of male scents that she had found so affecting before seemed even more disturbing at such close quarters. Her senses reacted violently to her situation and she was distractingly aware of the lean warmth of the body that half-supported her.

His voice too was a further distraction. Being so close he had no need to raise it above a murmur close to her ear, and it sent a series of little shivers along her spine each time he pointed out some fresh place of interest, so that only part of her attention was given to the places she was seeing, while the rest of her tried hard to resist the clamour of excitement aroused by her companion.

'The Mocenigo Palaces.' Carlo pointed to some elegant sixteenth-century buildings on the right bank. 'Your English Lord Byron once lived there; did you know that?'

From his voice she thought he expected her to be ignorant of the fact, and Sara turned her head to admit it. But that smiling dark face was much too close for comfort and she quickly turned away again, her reply part defensive and partly an attempt to calm the racing urgency of her heartbeat.

'Byron lived in so many places, I can't be expected to remember them all!' She laughed a little breathlessly and glanced at him briefly through her lashes. 'And he was only half English, you know. The other half was Scottish, like me.'

'So?' Carlo's voice breathed softly against her neck, his dark eyes glittering with laughter that teased her as well as tempted her to enlighten him further about her own ancestry. A long finger stroked back the honey-fair hair from her neck. 'You are not the English rose, *no*? You have the prickly Scottish thistle to lend an edge to your softness.'

'Prickly?' She questioned his opinion breathlessly, no longer taking an interest in the passing scene, but looking at him from the shadow of her lashes. '*Am* I prickly?'

'When you are indignant, and sure you are right about something—*si, mia cara*, you are very prickly, as I know to my cost!'

'Oh, that!' She shook her head to dismiss the initial cause of their meeting—the reproduction Urbino jug. 'I thought we'd agreed to bury that hatchet!'

'Ah, *si*! So we did, I am sorry.' He raised her hand to his lips and kissed the finger-tips lightly. 'We will not mention it ever again! Now things are different, *si*? You no longer—dislike me?'

The warmth of his body close to hers was like a charge of electricity, a stunning masculine assault on her senses that she was powerless to do anything about. He kept his hold on her hand and his strong hard fingers played with hers, gently but with a disturbing sensuality in their touch.

'I—I don't dislike you, Carlo.' She sought hard to

steady her voice, but it was still low and husky and quite unlike her usual one. 'I don't think I ever did—not actively dislike you.'

A gentle finger brushed her neck, moving aside the long silky hair while he pressed his lips to her warm soft skin. 'You are happy, *mia bella*, eh?'

Sara's heart was thudding wildly. It was impossible to remain cool and calm in the circumstances and she had to keep reminding herself how foolish it would be to let herself fall in love with a man like Carlo Cantorini. But he could disturb her at any time and in the present situation his proximity was devastating. Desperately she sought for a way to bring her wayward senses under control and made a determined effort to concentrate on the buildings that enhanced both banks of the waterway.

'Where are we now?' she asked, and sensed a momentary hesitation before Carlo answered her.

'Palazzo Madonnetta, one of the oldest *palazzi* in Venice. Built in Venetian-Byzantine style, it dates back to the twelfth and thirteenth centuries.'

The precise and historically accurate answer, delivered in a cool and very formal voice, made her realise how very obviously she had avoided answering his question, and she looked at him in sudden anxiety. 'You—you sound like a professional guide!' She laughed a little shakily and Carlo's dark eyes challenged her from the shadow of black lashes.

'I thought perhaps it was your wish that I should be nothing more than a guide, Sara.'

The coolness of his voice hurt more than she would have believed possible and she turned slightly more towards him, her hands over his where it lay on his lap, pressing the brown fingers anxiously. 'Oh, Carlo, please don't let's quarrel. Not now—not today when I'm enjoying myself so much!'

For a breathlessly anxious moment she feared he was not going to be persuaded, but then suddenly he smiled, a slightly wry smile that gave a crooked look to his mobile mouth, but which warmed the dark eyes encouragingly.

'*Benissimo, bella mia*, I will not spoil your enjoyment.' He looked down at her steadily for a few moments, then once more raised her hands to his lips. 'Today I am yours to command, *bella* Sara.'

It was a mood Sara had not encountered in him before, and she shook her head slowly, her laugh husky and uncertain. 'Oh no, you'll have to take command. I haven't the remotest idea where we're going even!'

'To Bennot's—a special place that I know where they make the most delicious *granita* in all Venice!'

'*Granita?*'

'Ice—the water-ice, *no*? Made with fresh fruit that Bennot buys himself from the market. I shall ask him to make yours with strawberries, *si*? You will love it!'

Quite convinced that she would love anything at all that he ordered for her, Sara laughed delightedly. 'Oh, I know I shall! And I've no doubt at all that I shall eat far too much again—I always do when I let you do the ordering for me!'

She hastily avoided his eyes when she realised how very intimate that had sounded, and Carlo's long finger stroked the back of her neck, persuasive and sensual, his voice close to her ear. 'Always, *cara?*'

'Well—twice, anyway!' She looked up at him, laughing still, her heart hammering with breathtaking urgency. 'You will translate the menu for me, won't you, Carlo?'

'*Naturalmente!*'

He held her gaze for so long that she felt the colour flood into her cheeks, and it was all she could do not to reach out and put her arms about him. The temptation to hug herself close to that irresistible masculine warmth burned in her like fire, and her own violent response to him stunned her.

He pressed both her hands in his one, his fingers hard and strong, and he murmured something in Italian which she did not understand, but it sounded so incredibly beautiful spoken in that soft deep voice that she smiled.

Sara's recollection of what followed was a little hazy and she was never quite certain how they came to be walking in a little park tucked away somewhere in the maze of Venetian canals and narrow, shadowed streets. They had crossed a couple of hump-backed bridges and wandered down several cool, dark *calles* after they left the restaurant, but she hadn't really taken note of where they were going.

Lunch had been long and leisurely, sitting at a discreet little table that overlooked the water, and she had felt almost deliriously lightheaded without the aid of the wine they had drunk with their meal. A selection of *antipasto* followed by deliciously tender veal served with eggs and cheese were only two of the courses she ate without really noticing what she was eating, and the famous water-ice came well up to the promise Carlo had made for it.

The idea of taking a casual stroll afterwards had been

by mutual consent, although Sara was prepared to follow any suggestion Carlo made. They had talked over lunch, touching briefly on quite a number of subjects, but conversation had taken second place to the sheer pleasure of being in his company, and she did not yet realise that she knew very little more about him now than she had when they first met. All she knew for certain was that she would find it impossible to ever see him in the same light again after today.

The park was small and very quiet. When they first arrived a family of four were the only other people in sight, walking along neat paths laid out between little patches of grass scattered with the unexpected familiarity of white daisies, just like the ones that grew on the lawn at home.

Unable to resist renewing a childish pleasure, she picked a handful of the little white blooms and strung them into a daisy chain, much to the delight of the two dark-eyed children walking with their parents. And the little girl danced off delightedly with the coronet of daisies encircling her shiny black hair.

'You like children?'

Carlo's quiet voice brought her round again after waving to the Italian family as they walked off in the opposite direction, and she laughed. She hadn't given the question much thought, but she supposed she did like children, especially if they were as dark-eyed and enchanting as the two who had just left them.

'Those two were very sweet,' she allowed, then laughed a little uncertainly and shrugged her shoulders. 'Yes, I suppose I do like children, but I find Italian *bambini* particularly adorable. It probably has something to do with those huge dark eyes.'

Carlo's dark eyes looked down at her, warm and smiling in that strong but gentle face. 'Ah, you have a liking for dark eyes, eh?'

'It seems so!' She glanced up at him, her mouth soft and half smiling; suddenly and inexplicably shy. 'I could well become addicted to Italy, and to Venice in particular!'

'You will stay here when your uncle returns?'

She had not really considered what she would do when her uncle came back from his honeymoon, and she found the question suddenly disturbing. Possibly she would be invited to stay on for a holiday; she hoped she would be, for she could not face the thought of leaving Venice at the moment.

'I hope I can stay for a while at least.' She must have betrayed something of what she was feeling in her voice, because Carlo was looking down at her more seriously and his hand on her arm tightened its hold slightly, pressing into her soft skin firmly. 'I—I hope he'll ask me to stay for a holiday.'

'I hope so too, *mia cara* Sara.'

They walked a little longer in silence, a strange kind of musing silence, as if both had something on their mind that needed serious thought. It was a moment or two before Carlo suddenly squeezed gently on her arm, and when she looked up at him he was smiling, one black brow arched questioningly. 'You enjoyed your lunch at Bennot's, Sara?'

It seemed he was making an attempt to recover that satisfying and delicate rapport that had so far made their time together so enjoyable, but somehow Sara feared it was not going to be quite the same again. For some reason she could not determine, mentioning her uncle's return and her own future plans had changed things.

'It was perfect, Carlo, thank you, especially that—*granita*?' He nodded approval of her accent. 'I've never tasted anything like it before.'

'It is also very good made with peaches. Next time you will try it, *si*?'

Next time. Her heart gave a sudden leap of excitement, and she glanced up at him through her lashes, wondering if he had meant her to take it as a promise. The little park was quiet now and they were alone, like two people on a small island surrounded by trees, and she felt quite suddenly and excitingly close to him.

There were two rather overgrown shrubs beside the path, forming a natural bower, and Carlo brought them to a halt beside it, drawing her into its shelter and looking down at her for a moment in silence. 'There will be a next time, eh, *piccola*?'

Sara's mouth trembled, soft and vulnerable with those steady dark eyes watching it so fixedly. 'I'd like it very much.'

'Sara——'

She was prepared for him taking her in his arms, but not for the urgent response of her own senses to the suggestion of passion his arms conveyed. He pulled her close, slowly at first, almost as if he feared the violence of his own emotions, then suddenly their bodies touched and it was like a fire consuming her.

His hands pressed her close, so close that she could feel every nerve in his body tensed like a coiled spring, every muscle straining her closer still, until his mouth, hard and demanding, parted her lips with bruising fierceness. Honey-fair hair was brushed aside by caressing fingers, and his lips pressed to her neck and the throbbing soft-ness of her throat, his voice murmuring in his own tongue, deep and lyrical as he whispered against her warm, scented skin.

Sara had never thought herself capable of wantonness, but in Carlo's arms she seemed to have no inhibitions. Lifting her arms, she drew his head down to her, her eyes closed as she pressed her lips to the raven's-wing of dark hair across his brow.

'Carlo!' She whispered his name and her fingers stroked his bowed head, her body responding urgently to those unfamiliar but incredibly exciting sensations he aroused in her. 'Carlo, Carlo!'

'*Bella mia!*' Large brown hands cupped her flushed face between them and he looked down into her eyes with an intensity that made her shiver. 'Oh, Sara, *bella* Sara!' He bent his head and once more that hard passionate mouth was on hers, sapping her resistence, making her forget everything but the wanton desires he aroused in her.

When he looked at her again, it was with a slightly wry look about the smile on his mouth and he studied her for a moment or two until she smiled at him in-quiringly. Then he kissed her mouth again lightly and a breath of deep laughter fluttered against her lips.

'When I first saw you, *cara mia*, I thought you a very self-sufficient and impudent young woman. Did you know that?'

Not at all surprised, Sara shook her head, smiling be-cause she knew his opinion had changed with her own of him. 'I thought it was something like that—you were very arrogant and sure of yourself!'

'So?' The hands on her shoulders stroked their way

down her bare arms with a sensual motion that was incredibly disturbing. 'I did not see you in those first few minutes—it was only when I saw you again on the bridge, lost and alone, that I realised what a lovely little creature you are!'

'Prickly?' she laughed, reminding him of their earlier conversation, and he shook his head.

'Sometimes, *piccola*, but I must know a lot more about you before I am qualified to give a true judgment on you as a woman.'

Her laughter was shiveringly unsteady, and she found it much too hard to meet his eyes when they watched her so intensely. With one finger she drew an imaginary line down the lapel of his jacket. 'You might be disappointed, Carlo.'

'Perhaps, but I do not think so.' A finger raised her chin, lifting her flushed face to look at him, and he held her gaze for a long moment before he spoke again. 'You will have lunch with me tomorrow too?'

It was as much statement as question, Sara realised, and she took a moment to realise how little he had changed. 'Tomorrow?'

The hand under her chin stroked persuasively back and forth while he looked down at her steadily. '*Si, cara mia.* Your uncle does not expect you to work without lunch, does he?'

'No, of course he doesn't!' Cris would make much of her seeing Carlo Cantorini in her lunch hour, she thought, so would Signora Vincenti; maybe even her uncle would not be in favour of her becoming so involved with a man of Carlo's reputation. But her own instinct was to follow her heart, and that led her to accepting without caring what anyone else said or thought. 'I usually go to a little *osteria* just across the square, and share a plate of *antipasto* with Cris, but——'

'So? He is important to you?' The black eyes challenged her and she hastily shook her head. 'Ah! Then tomorrow you will desert this—Cris?—and lunch with me, *si*?'

It was hard to believe that he did not know exactly what her answer was going to be, and yet the half smile with which he waited for her to answer showed a hint of uncertainty. It was an unexpected and very human doubt that made her feel strangely protective—a reaction she would not have believed possible only a few days ago. Twice today he had showed her that touching and unexpectedly vulnerable side to his character, and she wondered if it was because she felt so close to him for a few moments that she detected it.

'Sara?'

His soft-voiced prompting brought her hastily back to earth and she looked up at him and smiled. 'I'll desert Cris and have lunch with you,' she promised, and Carlo reached out his arms for her again.

'*Bene*,' he said softly.

CHAPTER EIGHT

NOTHING was as usual the following morning. Sara had woken with the feeling that everything was as near perfect as it could be for her, and she had no idea that anything was amiss until she went in for breakfast and found Signora Vincenti with red-rimmed eyes and weeping noisily as she prepared breakfast. Her husband apparently saw Sara's appearance as a godsend, and he hurried out of the house, leaving his wife to explain the reason for her tears.

In a spate of Italian and barely intelligible English, Signora Vincenti told her that her *bambino*, her Crispino, had run away from his *màmma* and broken her heart. Cris had not come home all night, and she was completely at a loss to know why he should have gone off like this. A brief telephone call to let her know that he was all right, was not enough; he was her *bambino* and she wanted him home.

Much as she sympathised, Sara was in something of a quandary. She could imagine who Cris was with, if not where they were, but she had promised Cris not to say anything about his Maria, and she was loth to break her word to him. He had let his mother know that he was all right, so there was no real need to concern herself, but she just wished he had chosen another time to make his gesture of defiance.

Coming as it did, it rather put a damper on her own happiness and she resented anything that spoiled her pleasant sense of satisfaction. If he did not come home by this evening she would tell them about Maria, but somehow she had a feeling that he would come to his senses before too long, and she would not have to break her word to him.

Consoling Signora Vincenti as best she could, she left her to go to the shop. Her uncle's business had to be carried on, no matter what traumas arose, and she set off alone, taking a *vaporetto* as a precaution against getting lost again. She still hesitated to find her way alone on foot and she could not guarantee that Carlo would be there again to rescue her.

It seemed a long, tiring morning, and only the thought of lunching with Carlo kept up her spirits as she coped with clients and book work as well as the jobs that Cris more usually did around the shop. Locking up at lunchtime, she was putting the key in her handbag when her wrist was seized and she was spun round quickly, only to be brought up short against the lean hardness of a masculine body that was excitingly familiar.

Startled for a moment, she rested her forehead against his chest, then looked up into the dark eyes gleaming with laughter, her mouth pouted in momentary reproach, the strong hard fingers holding her head to the steady beat of his heart.

'*Buon giorno*, Sara!'

He did not kiss her, but the look in his eyes was like a caress and he pursed his mouth slightly as he looked down at her, sending little shivers of anticipation through her whole body so that she laughed to cover the sudden excitement she felt at being close to him again. Looking back over his shoulder as they moved off along the street, Carlo raised an inquiring brow at her.

'Has your young assistant already gone?'

Sara had forgotten Cris's absence for a second or two and she pulled a face when she was reminded. She loved the familiarity of Carlo holding her hand as they walked along, but if she let the recurring thought of Cris intrude it could spoil their lunch together, and she was determined not to let that happen.

She shrugged, her voice deliberately casual. 'He's gone —quite literally.' Seeing his puzzled frown, she hastened to explain. 'Cris didn't come home last night.'

'Oh? There is—trouble?'

She took it that he meant family trouble, and shook her head firmly. 'Oh no, there's nothing like that; they're a happy enough family on the whole, even if Signor Vincenti is——' She shrugged and laughed a little uncertainly, remembering the roving eye and determined charm of Cris's father. 'Oh no, there's nothing at home to make Cris want to leave.'

'Ah! He is simply—trying his wings, *no?*'

He dismissed it as unimportant, and it was clear he was far more interested in their lunch together, so that Sara was willing enough to put Cris to the back of her mind for the moment. Nothing more was said about the matter until they were almost finished their meal, and then Sara glanced at her watch, realising that she still had a business to run, no matter how unwelcome the fact was at the moment. She was going to have to cope alone, at least until Cris came to his senses.

But brief as it was the gesture did not go unnoticed, and Carlo was looking across at her, questioning her apparent haste. 'Are you impatient to leave, Sara?'

'No, not at all!' She hastened to deny it, anxious that he should believe her. 'I wish I didn't have to hurry, but without Cris it's going to be rather hectic for me on my own. I don't know how long he's likely to be gone.'

'You do not anticipate that he will stay away then, huh?'

Sara wished she could be more sure. She could not imagine two such young people having much chance to hide for very long with no means of support, and the girl at least was probably already having second thoughts. For a moment she pondered on the wisdom of telling Carlo about Maria, but she wondered if he would understand her willingness to keep Cris's secret, even if she was having thoughts about telling his mother.

On the whole she thought he was likely to take the strictly Italian view of a young girl running off with her boy-friend, no matter how young he might be, and she shook her head. 'I don't know,' she confessed. 'I think he'll probably see how wrong he is in time.'

Carlo was eyeing her curiously, she thought, almost as if he suspected she knew the reason for Cris having left home, as if he suspected there was a little more to it than simply a young man trying his wings. 'He is—doing wrong?'

Sara hastily shook her head. 'Oh no, not—not really.'

'Sara?'

It was an invitation to confide, she knew, and she would have done without hesitation had it not been for that promise to Cris. If he did not return by this evening she would tell Signora Vincenti about it, but not yet— she couldn't tell anyone yet. She shook her head once more and looked down at the wine glass she held rather than at Carlo.

'I just wish he knew how much trouble he's causing, that's all. Boys can be very selfish and thoughtless.'

The gleam in his eyes suggested laughter rather than

sympathy, and he held his wine glass between long brown fingers as he regarded her steadily. 'How old is this—miscreant, Sara, eh?'

'Nearly seventeen. I know,' she added hastily, 'he's more a young man than a boy, but it doesn't stop his mother worrying about him.'

'*Naturalmente*, but a young man always causes heartache when he is growing up, Sara, that is the way of things.'

It seemed such a callous way to dismiss poor Signora Vincenti's tears, and Sara's reaction was instinctively defensive. She had seen the Signora's red-rimmed eyes and unhappy face, Carlo hadn't. No matter if Cris was almost a young man, it did not give him the right to cause such heartache, whatever Carlo's opinion.

'That's something you'd know more about than I do, of course!'

She was sorry she had said it, even before the words were out of her mouth, but the steady dark gaze from across the table did not waver, and she hastily lowered her eyes before it. Carlo reached out and pressed her hand. 'Why should it trouble *you* so much, Sara?'

His voice suggested impatience, as if he suspected her more personally involved than she admitted, and Sara once more resented Cris's ill-timed gesture of independence. The last thing she wanted was for her and Carlo to disagree about Cris, and she smiled ruefully, her eyes appealing for understanding.

'I'm sorry, Carlo; but he's Signora Vincenti's youngest, and she dotes on him rather. She was so upset this morning that I didn't like leaving her.'

Dark eyes, shadowed by black lashes, swept over her face slowly and came to rest on the vulnerable softness of her mouth. 'You have too much heart, *mia cara*. This young man is not your personal concern, is he?'

'No, of course not.' She sighed, glancing at her watch again. 'But it does mean I have everything to do on my own, Carlo.'

'So be it!'

It was clear that he did not like the idea of her wanting to go so soon, but he called for the waiter to bring their bill and watched her steadily while they waited for him to come over. When something did not please him he could look dismayingly autocratic, and he did so now, so that she had no doubt he did not want her to go.

It gave her a curious fluttering sensation when she realised it and she looked at him from the shadow of her lashes, her voice strangely breathless when she spoke. 'I'm sorry I have to rush off, Carlo, but you must understand how it is, with Cris not being there to help.'

He made no effort to hide his resentment, and she wondered if it was pleasure in her company that made him resent her departure or simply that he was unused to having his luncheon dates cut short by the woman he was lunching with.

'I do not like being abandoned, *mia cara*, in favour of a—a shop. I will be more pleased when your uncle returns from his *luna di miele*, then you will not have to make such haste to leave me!'

It was an arrogant remark, but Sara had long since admitted his arrogance as part of his attraction; it was her own feelings that troubled her most. She wished she was better able to accept that his present desire for her company was unlikely to be permanent.

She should be able to face the fact that the present state of affairs was merely a pleasant interlude, one of many as far as Carlo was concerned, and that no one need be hurt when it ended. Instead she clung to every moment with him, fearful it might be her last, and her hands trembled as she gathered up her handbag.

He had known many rich and beautiful women, and it was difficult sometimes to believe that she had moved into such select company. Not so difficult to remember the bitterness and anger of that dark, sophisticated woman at the restaurant he had taken her to that first evening, or Signora Vincenti's opinion of him as a breaker of hearts.

She laughed a little unsteadily, her hands on the clasp of her bag. 'He won't be back for a week or two yet, Carlo. You may get tired of waiting.'

Her heart fluttered anxiously when she saw the way he was frowning at her, and after a moment he leaned across the table towards her. He looked into her eyes, his own dark and glittering, and his straight firm mouth unsmiling as he reached long hard fingers for her hand and pressed it almost painfully hard.

'That is foolish, *piccola*, as you know well enough, *si*?'

It was difficult to even hold his gaze, her senses responded so violently to the touch of those strong fingers, and she shook her head after a second, looking down at his hand. The waiter hovered nearby, close enough to make her aware of him, and she glanced at him swiftly before shaking her head.

Following her gaze briefly, Carlo half-smiled, then raised her hand and pressed his lips to her fingers, apparently undisturbed by the man's proximity. For a second his dark eyes gleamed at her with that slightly malicious laughter that she had seen in both Gianni and Signor Cantorini at various times.

'You blush so enchantingly, *carissima*—forgive me, *no?*'

Fortunately the afternoon proved much less hectic than the morning had been and Sara had time to dwell on her own situation now and then. She had little doubt that she was on the very brink of being in love with Carlo, but at the moment she was too uncertain about anything to know what she could do about it.

It was well into the afternoon when the door opened and she looked up, the smile she had ready wavering when Carlo came in to the shop, looking so unmistakably angry that she was reminded of the very first time they met. Then he had come storming into the shop demanding the return of his property; heaven knew what had brought him here in such a passion today.

From just the other side of the counter he regarded her for a moment or two in silence and his dark eyes glittered a challenge just as they had that first time. His change of mood was so startlingly different from when he had left her at the door only a couple of hours earlier that she looked at him anxiously.

'Carlo, what on earth's the matter?'

She had a strong desire to reach out and touch him, as if physical contact would avert his anger, for it became clear when he spoke that it was directed at her. 'I have said that one of the things I like about you is that you are honest, is that not right, Sara?'

'Why—yes.' Her head was spinning as she tried to fathom what on earth could have brought him to her in this disturbingly violent mood. 'But—why——'

'You told me about the young man who works here with you; at lunch time, *si?*' She nodded, too stunned to answer, and he went on in a flat hard voice that dismayed her without her being quite sure why. 'You did know not why he had left his home, eh, Sara?'

'I—I don't——'

'Tell me, *mia cara* Sara, does he have an *amante*, this young man whose mother weeps for him?'

Sara felt a sudden cold sensation in her stomach, and she licked her lips anxiously as she nodded. 'Yes—at least, not exactly a lover——'

'A sweetheart, Sara, that is the sense in this instant!' His eyes gleamed at her in such a way that she felt herself trembling with the reaction his violence aroused. 'You remember Maria Laurana, of course?' His voice was carefully under control, flat and precise and dismayingly cold. 'You were at the villa at Gianni's invitation when you met her, were you not? And Maria's arrival was an unexpected—complication, eh? Of course you remember her, Sara!'

'Carlo, I really don't see why you're—why you're telling me this.'

But she did, Sara thought with growing conviction, and prayed she was wrong. *'Dio mio!'* Carlo swore softly, as if he did not want to admit whatever it was that troubled him so much. 'To think that you sat with me and looked into my eyes while all the time—*Santa Madre!* I believed you as innocent as your face!'

'Carlo!'

His dark eyes held hers determinedly, glittering like jet in the yellow shop lights, and she knew why he was so angry, that made it worse. 'You did not mention why this young man left his home, did you, Sara?' She hastily avoided his eyes, looking instead at her own restless hands on the counter-top. 'Ah!' He pounced on her hasty evasion at once. 'But you do know why he ran off, do you not, *ragazza mia*?'

She knew very well, Sara thought despairingly, but Maria had seemed such an ordinary name in a country like Italy, and the significance had not even struck her. Carlo reached across for her hands, not gently this time, but with a cruelly hard grip, his mouth set tight, as if he hated her deception above everything else, and she pulled back against his hold instinctively.

'Maria Laurana's parents came to me because they suspected at first that she might have gone with Gianni. She has been missing from home since last night—does that not strike you as significant, Sara?' She was shaking her head, but he pulled her towards him, his eyes bright and almost black in the yellow lighting. 'You knew it was Maria Laurana this young man had gone away with, did you not?'

'Carlo——'

'You left me in no doubt that you did not approve of the plan for Gianni to marry Maria. Did you see this as an opportunity to put a stop to that plan?' He gave her no time to answer but shook his head impatiently, his grip cruelly tight as he held her still. '*Dio mio*, it is the thought of you lying to me that I hate so much!'

He was hurting her probably more than he realised, and she tried again to free herself, looking at him anxiously. 'Carlo, I didn't know!'

'Do not lie any more, Sara, it is not like you. Or perhaps I do not know you as I thought I did!'

'You don't know me at all if you believe me capable of such a—a deception!'

He seemed less violently angry now, even resigned, and his voice had a depth that suggested disillusion. 'Do you think I do not remember how you answered when I gave you the opportunity to tell me why this boy had gone away? You looked away, Sara, you avoided my eyes and you denied he had done any wrong.'

She managed at last to free her hands and stood rubbing the marks on her wrists left by his gripping fingers. Her voice husky with the threat of tears as she tried to explain. 'I'd no idea Cris was seeing Maria Laurana, Carlo. I knew he had a—girlfriend, but——'

'He did not mention her name?'

Sara felt cornered, anxious and defensive, pleading her own cause far more earnestly than Cris's, but she had to tell him the truth, nothing else even entered her head. 'I knew her name was Maria.'

'Ah!'

He put such satisfaction in to that short, sharp sound that she could almost believe he enjoyed it, and her heart leapt urgently as she put in her own defence. 'Maria is a common enough name, Carlo! Cris used to see her on the way home; we pass the Convent of Santa Amelia and he told me she was a pupil there, but I never even knew which one she was. He used to just—look at her at first. It was later that he told me he'd spoken to her.'

How could she tell him the rest? Sara thought wildly. Evading his eyes, she rubbed at the marks on her wrists. 'He—he said something about her parents making her marry someone, and that if they did, they—Cris and Maria, would——' She looked up at him, shaking her head. 'I didn't take any of it seriously, I just thought it was—talk. And I'd no idea it was Maria Laurana he was talking about.'

Carlo's eyes still glowed darkly from the other side of

the counter, though he was definitely less passionately angry than he had been. 'Would you have told me today at lunchtime, if you had known, Sara? Or would you have encouraged them to go against Maria's parents because you did not agree with the idea yourself?'

Challenged so directly, Sara lifted her chin. Threatening tears gave a misty look to her grey eyes, but there was anger too in her. He had hurt her, more than she would have believed possible, but in her anger she wanted to hit back before she made a complete fool of herself and burst into tears.

'You found the idea of Cris—spreading his wings quite amusing when you heard about it,' she reminded him, choking on those persistent tears. 'It's different now that you think it can spoil your marriage plans for Gianni, isn't it, Carlo? You're angry about it so you just—hit out! You hit out and you don't care who you hurt!'

'Sara——'

His voice was still edged with the hardness of anger, but there might have been a glimpse of uncertainty in his eyes, an expression that suggested he might be regretting some of the things he had said to her. But Sara was too disturbed, too hurt to think of being amenable, and she cut across whatever it was he had been going to say, her own voice small and unsteady, but insistent.

'I don't know where Cris and Maria are, but even if I did I don't think I'd tell you, Carlo. I doubt very much if you know very much about love, even puppy-love!'

His reply was short and virulent, and in his own tongue, and Sara felt as if she had been drained of every vestige of hope as he turned swiftly and went striding out of the shop, just as he had that first time he came. Only this time Sara watched him go with a heavy heart and eyes that were already filling with tears, and when he went past the window without even glancing through it, she covered her face with her hands and wept.

Sara was never quite sure how she got through the remainder of the day. She had never felt more miserable and confused in her life, and it did little to console her that she was at least in part to blame for the situation she now found herself in. For sure Carlo had berated her unfairly, but she had rejected the signs of reconciliation just before he left, and been as hurtful to him in turn.

She closed the shop rather earlier than usual and was walking across the little square to where the *vaporetti* started from when she caught sight of a familiar figure leaning against the wall on the corner of the street she had to take to the canal. Too surprised for a second or two to do other than stare, she hastily pulled herself together and hurried across, half afraid that Cris would disappear before she got to him.

He made no move to go, however, but simply looked up at her with an air of mingled embarrassment and defiance, as if he was very unsure of his reception, and Sara tried to think of something to say to him that would not embarrass him further. She felt angry in the first instance, that he should have been the cause of so much trouble to everyone, not least herself, but then those dark, appealing eyes won her over and she placed a hand on his arm.

Cris hauled himself away from the wall and rubbed one hand on the back of his head, a faint hint of a smile flashing over his shoulder at her as they walked off together. He looked quite bright as if he had nothing in the world to worry about, and it crossed Sara's mind that

Carlo was probably right. Other hearts might ache, but young men like Cris came through the process of trying their wings practically unscathed.

'If you're coming home with me, I might as well walk,' she said, and marvelled at the matter-of-factness of her own voice.

Cris said nothing for a moment, but thrust his hands into his pockets and swung along with a vaguely defiant step, his head downbent, watching his own feet. They were part way across a bridge when he turned, half-turning his head and smiling, seeking her response, and so appealing that there was only one way she could respond.

'What happened, Cris? Where's Maria?'

He shrugged lightly, though she felt it was not as careless as it appeared. 'At home with her *màmma*.'

She almost sighed aloud in relief, though heaven knew why it should concern her so closely. 'Oh, Cris, why did you do it?'

'*Non so.*' He was unsure of himself and he spoke Italian, she suspected because it came easiest to him at such a moment.

'Didn't you realise the trouble you'd cause?'

'Màmma?' He looked sheepish, but shrugged once more as if it was something he preferred not to think about too deeply. 'I think Màmma will forgive me when she knows how it was.'

That was something that had yet to be discovered, she realised, and looked at him anxiously. 'How was it, Cris?'

He said nothing for a few seconds, then spoke without looking at her, watching his feet instead as he walked along beside her. 'Maria had told her parents that she was to visit an old aunt. As it happened, she did so, and I spent the night on a seat in a *parco*.' He looked at her with a hint of a smile on his mouth. 'It was very uncomfortable, you will be pleased to know.'

'You could have come home, didn't you think of that?'

Again those eloquent young shoulders heaved, and he pulled a wry face. '*Sì*, I thought of it, but—it was all such a mistake, Sara, I did not know how to tell anyone.'

'Maria got frightened?'

She had guessed correctly, she saw by his quick glance over his shoulders. 'Maria is a child,' he decreed firmly, and Sara tried not to smile, even though she realised how in vain all her arguing with Carlo had been.

'Of course, she is, Cris, and so are you!' She shook her head, denying herself the right to scold him, though she felt like doing so when she thought of all the trouble he had caused, simply to find out that his convent schoolgirl was just that. 'But it's not my place to tell you off, that's your mother's job, she's been worried sick about you.'

Once more he seemed very sure of his mother's forgiveness, and he was probably quite right. 'Màmma will understand and not blame me too much. There is no harm done, *no*?'

'Isn't there?' He turned swiftly, obviously recognising a new tone in her voice but unable to see a reason for it. 'Didn't you realise that your Maria is—well, that Gianni Cantorini is the man her parents want her to marry?'

'*Sì*, I know it since last night. It is one reason why I did not wish to insist on Maria staying with me, you understand?'

'Oh, I understand perfectly, Cris!' There was nothing she could do about the bitterness in her voice. 'The only trouble is that Carlo—Signor Carlo Cantorini didn't believe me when I said I hadn't any idea that your Maria and the girl he hopes will marry his son were one and the same girl.'

'Oh, *màmma mia!*' He rolled his expressive eyes heavenwards. 'Oh, Sara, have I made trouble for you?'

'I'm afraid you have!' She laughed bitterly when she remembered how she and Carlo had parted just a little time ago. 'Carlo is under the impression that I knew all about it and that I encouraged you to run off with her.'

'You have quarrelled?' His huge dark eyes were disturbingly knowing as he looked round at her, and she could do nothing about the faint flush that coloured her cheeks. 'I am sorry, Sara.'

'So am I!' She had not meant it to sound quite so rueful and once more she felt his eyes on her, assessing the effect it had had on her because she had quarrelled with Carlo Cantorini. 'I think—I have the feeling that he's as much upset because he thinks I deceived him as because Maria went off with you.'

'So?' Cris might be little more than a boy, but she had the discomfiting feeling that he understood Carlo's motives as well, or better, than she did herself, and he was watching her face as he walked beside her along another narrow *calle* that led to the next bridge. 'It matters to you that you have quarrelled with Signor Carlo Cantorini, Sara?'

'It matters.' She might as well admit it, Sara thought, for she had the feeling that Cris knew exactly how much it mattered. 'I don't like being put into a position like that, Cris.'

'I am sorry.'

Something occurred to her then, and she turned and looked at him curiously. 'Why haven't you been home yet, Cris?'

He cast a swift, half defiant glance from the corners of his eyes, and a faint smile fluttered around his mobile mouth. 'I wished to come home when you did, Sara, so that you——'

'So that I'd put in a word for you!' She shook her head slowly. 'I don't see how that's going to help, Cris.'

'Oh, Sara! *Per favore, si?*' That half smile with the appeal in those dark eyes was irresistible, and she knew she would do as he said without even stopping to think about it. 'Then maybe I can appeal for you to Signor Cantorini, eh?'

'Oh no, please don't!' She curled inside to think of him pleading with Carlo on her behalf, and she looked at him earnestly as they crossed the hump-backed bridge together. 'Promise me you won't, please Cris.'

Cris shrugged, his eyes darkly speculative. '*Si, benissimo,*' he agreed after a moment or two. 'I promise that I will not say anything to Signor Carlo Cantorini about this. O.K.?'

'O.K.' He really was irresistible, Sara thought, and admired Maria Laurana's powers of resistance, even though she had Gianni Cantorini as an alternative. Smiling in response to the saucy wink he gave her, she shook her head. 'I ought really to be angry with you, you know, not plead for you with your mother.'

Cris laughed, taking her arm in a gesture of impudent familiarity, and she somehow felt less downhearted herself when she heard it. There was something irrepressible about Cris that made it hard not to forgive him anything. She trusted him not to say anything to Carlo—that was something she would have to sort out for herself, provided she was given the opportunity.

CHAPTER NINE

SARA was rather surprised to see Gianni come into the shop the following morning, only she could not help wishing that it was Carlo who had come instead. Not that she expected to see him again after the way they had parted yesterday, but somewhere deep down in her heart she had hoped he would.

She expected some sign of indignation from Gianni too, but he seemed more or less as usual as he smiled at her. A little more serious than was customary, perhaps, but his hazel eyes still showed appreciation at the sight of her, and he smiled readily. He cast a brief glance at the curtain that concealed the entrance to the back room before he spoke, and raised an inquiring brow.

'*Buon giorno,* Sara. Are you alone?'

She was thankful to be able to confirm it in the circumstances, and Sara nodded. 'Cris is out on an errand at the moment. Good morning, Gianni.'

She regarded him with a hint of wariness, for it was obvious that he had something on his mind, and she had little doubt that it was to do with Cris and Maria. Maybe he shared some of his father's suspicions regarding her own part in the affair, and she was prepared to defend herself as firmly as she had yesterday with Carlo.

Leaning on the counter he seemed quite at ease for all his air of seriousness. 'You are troubled about what happened between Maria and—your friend, hmm?' A hand enclosed her own and squeezed encouragingly, but he gave her no time to confirm or deny it. 'But no harm was done, Sara, and you are in no way to blame for them going away.'

'I had no idea, I promise you, even though Ca——' She shrugged uneasily without mentioning Carlo's suspicions, though she had a fair idea that Gianni probably knew about that too.

'This is not the dark ages, *cara*! I will not blame Maria for behaving so foolishly, I promise you. It was a—a gesture, no more!'

'But it could have been serious, Gianni, we have to face that fact. It was silly and selfish!' She was thinking mostly of the rift it had caused between herself and Carlo and she spoke with more passion than she realised.

'So!' Gianni shrugged philosophically, though it couldn't be that he did not realise the possibilities of what had happened. 'He is no fool that one, I think, *si*?'

'Cris?'

She looked at him curiously, wondering at his confident assessment. His mouth showed a hint of that same wry smile that sometimes characterised his father's amusement. 'Crispino Vincenti has discovered what I have known for some time,' he informed her with remarkable coolness. 'He has learned that Maria is still a convent schoolgirl and not yet ready to be a woman. Also I think he was influenced by the fact that it was Giovanni Cantorini whom her family wish her to marry. As I say, he is not a fool, that one!'

'Gianni, how did you find out all this? Not from Maria?'

'No, no, no!' The idea seemed briefly to amuse him, and after what he had just said about Maria she could understand him finding it amusing. 'Maria would not tell me such things, I have not even seen her. But I have seen Crispino Vincenti.'

Sara's heart gave a sudden lurch and almost stifled her with the urgency of its beat as she stared at him in dismay. Gianni, on the other hand, seemed to be taking it all in his stride and he was leaning forward with an elbow on the counter top, and one hand enclosing hers, squeezing her fingers gently.

'He told me how he and Maria met, and why they went away.' His lower lip curled in a hint of disdain, and he laughed. 'If one can look upon such an effort as running away. They did not even leave Venice! Hah! Children!'

Sara could understand his reaction to some extent, for he was so much more worldly than Cris, even though there was little more than a couple of years between them, but she wondered if he realised how fortunate it was that Cris and Maria were such children.

'It's lucky they are, Gianni, but——' She looked at him earnestly. 'You said Cris told you——'

'Si, mia cara, he came to the villa last night to see us.'

By us, Sara automatically assumed that he included Carlo, and she looked at him in dismay, a hot colour flooding her cheeks as she visualised Carlo listening to Cris's explanation and believing that she knew he was coming to make it.

'Oh no!' she said huskily, and Gianni gave her a curious look and frowned. 'Oh, Gianni, I asked him—I begged him not to!'

'But I am pleased that he did, bella mia. He explained how troubled you were because Carlo blamed you for what happened.'

'He didn't blame me, only thought I knew about it and didn't tell him.'

Her defence of Carlo was swift and instinctive and Gianni noted it with an arched brow. 'Whatever the truth, *cara*, Nonno was very impressed by this young man's devotion to you.'

'He saw Signor Cantorini too?' Her heart was thudding hard when she looked up into his face. 'Gianni, was——'

'Carlo was not at home, Sara, but I believe Nonno will tell him of Crispino's visit when he comes home this morning.'

It shouldn't hurt quite so much, Sara thought, but it did. It could not possibly be the first time that Carlo had spent a night away from home and she should be able to take it as a matter of course, just as Gianni did.

'You—you haven't seen him this morning?'

Gianni's hazel eyes were steady, searching and speculative, as Carlo's so often were. 'No, *cara mia*, but when he returns and he learns how unhappy you are because you have quarrelled, he will come and see you.'

'Oh, but I'm sure he won't!'

She realised how much her voice trembled when Gianni's hand stroked soothingly against her cheek, and he lifted her face, smiling as he looked down at her. 'You do not know him well if you think that, Sara. His anger is impulsive, he acts—on the spur of the moment?—is that right?'

'That's right, but it doesn't sound like Carlo.'

'But it is, Sara, I tell you the truth. Many times Carlo has acted so, and so often been sorry afterwards that he was so impulsive.'

It was just possible, Sara mused. For it had surely been

an impulsive gesture that had brought him to the Vincenti home that evening he took her to dinner in Gianni's stead; and when he had kissed her so unexpectedly and so fervently immediately before she fled from the Villa Cantorini because she was too unsure of his motives.

'You know that my mother was English?'

The unexpected question brought her swiftly back to earth and she nodded, not quite sure what subject he was following now. 'You told me that the first time we met,' she reminded him.

'Ah! But that will serve to show you just how impulsive Carlo can be, Sara. It was an impulse that he married my *màmma*.'

So many times Sara had wished she knew about Carlo's wife—what she had been like, how he came to meet her, but now that Gianni was about to tell her she felt strangely guilty about hearing it without Carlo's knowledge. Despite his very active social life, he had always struck her as a very private man who valued his privacy, and she shook her head before Gianni went further.

'Gianni, I'm not sure——'

'Oh, but *certamente* you must hear about my *màmma*, Sara! It is not secret, although it is not talked of often. Carlo was only eighteen years when they met; it was what you call a holiday romance, *si*? They met, the young English girl and Carlo, and they were young and it was summer and——' He used his hands to convey his meaning with such explicitness that Sara felt herself flush. 'They were married, though Nonno would have had them wait for a while, and then I am coming and it is not so *romantica*, eh?'

She could imagine, Sara thought, all too clearly. Two eighteen-year-olds with their eyes full of stars and suddenly brought down to earth by the prospect of parenthood. 'They parted?' she guessed, and Gianni nodded.

'She is too English, you understand, she does not like to live in Italy, and as soon as I am born she leaves me with Carlo and Nonno, and goes home. On the way home she was involved in a crash and killed.'

'Oh, Gianni, what a tragedy! At eighteen!'

'*Sì!*'

It was much too remote for Gianni to feel anything, but Sara's thoughts were with Carlo. An eighteen-year-old boy, suddenly widowed and left with a baby son to bring up; no wonder Carlo Cantorini was so wary of marrying again. The wonder was that he was not bitter as well as wary. She looked up at Gianni and shook her head slowly, unsure just what she could say next.

'I'm glad you've told me, Gianni, but I'm not sure you should have done; not without Carlo's knowledge.'

'Oh, but he will not mind that, you know, Sara.'

'The way things are at the moment?' She pulled a face and laughed rather unsteadily. 'I think he would.'

'Have I not said that he will come and see you just as soon as he returns? He will, Sara, you will see.'

She felt strangely uneasy suddenly, as if none of it was quite real. She wanted so much to believe that Carlo would come and see her again, as Gianni said, this time seeking a reconciliation instead of in anger, but she found it hard to imagine him even bothering about her if he was so taken up with another woman. And she felt very sure that he had found someone else, another distraction such as she had been herself lately.

'We'll see.' She laughed and drew back from the stroking hand on her cheek. 'Anyway, I'm glad to see you again, Gianni, and I'm more than glad that things are still all right between you and Maria.'

'You are interested in me and Maria?'

She looked at him uncertainly for a moment, trying to fathom just what lay behind that softly-spoken and rather enigmatic question. Then she nodded slowly, a half smile barely touching her lips. 'Well—yes. You do—like her, don't you, Gianni?'

'*Si*, I like her, *bella* Sara.'

It was a delicate matter to approach with any confidence, but she wanted to know because to some extent it concerned Carlo. It could be that Cris's escapade had put paid once and for all to Carlo's plans for his son, and it seemed to matter a great deal somehow that things should work out as he wanted them to. Gianni, she thought, knew what was on her mind, for he was smiling and shaking his head, looking at her with a hint of mischief in his eyes.

'Almost certainly I shall be married to Maria in time,' he said. 'That is what Carlo and Nonno want, and Maria's parents too—it would please everyone.'

'And you?'

She had to ask, and Gianni was smiling. 'I also, Sara. I am very fond of Maria, though she is rather too much the schoolgirl at the moment for my taste.' He rolled his eyes in a way that to Sara was so typically Italian she could not help smiling. 'But she will grow up in time, *si*? I will teach her to be a woman!'

'But gently, Gianni, she's very young!'

Heaven knew why she had felt the need to speak for Maria, except that she thought she might do something to influence him towards being more concerned about her feelings. Gianni, however, was watching her slightly flushed face with quizzical eyes that saw much more than she wanted him to.

'She is the same age as my *màmma* was when she had me, *cara*.'

She had forgotten the very young and ill-fated Signora Cantorini for a moment, and she shook her head to dismiss a rather discomfiting ghost. 'Yes, I know,' she said.

'You misjudge me, Sara.' He leaned across and stroked her cheek before kissing her lightly, his voice soft and quiet, more like Carlo's than she had ever heard it before. 'As you misjudge my father, I think, *mia cara*. It is very different with those we love, as you will discover.'

'Gianni——'

His thumb pressed lightly over her lips and he smiled, and it struck her suddenly how much more mature he was than she had realised. 'I must leave you, *bella* Sara, for I am seeing Maria and her *màmma* for luncheon.' He pulled a face, though his eyes had a deep warm glow in his darkly good-looking face. 'I must let her see that I forgive her, *sì*?'

'Oh, Gianni!' She was smiling, reaching up to touch his face and almost loving him without for a moment being in love with him. 'You're the nicest man I know.'

'*Sì, naturalmente!*' His smile teased her, and he leaned across the counter once more to press a kiss on her mouth, then laughed as he turned away. 'You have good taste, *bella mia*—to choose a Cantorini to love!'

He was gone before Sara could fully grasp the significance of what he had said, and she watched him go past the window in a kind of daze, waving a hand automatically in response to his impudent salute. Gianni knew; he had recognised it even before she was quite certain herself just how she felt about Carlo, and she wished with all her heart she could do something to change things. Only she had the feeling that it was already too late.

It was close on three o'clock when the shop door opened and Sara caught her breath, totally unprepared to find Carlo looking across at her. In a light suit with a silk shirt and a tie he looked very virile and exciting as well as businesslike, and Sara's whole being responded to him with alarming urgency.

He did not move from the doorway, but stood lean and dark as a panther, just inside the door until she smiled, a little tremulously. Then he came across on those familiar long easy strides until the counter brought him up short and he stood looking down at her, his dark eyes lingering on the softness of her mouth.

'Carlo, I have to——'

She broke off when he spoke at the exact same moment, saying the same words except that he used her name, and she felt a curious churning sensation in her stomach when he leaned across the glass-topped counter suddenly and kissed her mouth, his lips lingering and reluctant to leave hers, while her heart raced like a wild thing, making her flushed and breathless.

'I have so little time!' He spoke softly and with a certain huskiness, sparing a glance for the clock on the wall behind her and frowning as if it annoyed him with its speedy second hand ticking round the shiny gold face. 'I have to go away for a few days, Sara, but I will see you when I come back, hmm? We will talk then.'

'You're going away?'

The anxiety she felt showed in her voice and Carlo smiled, showing strong white teeth in the darkness of his face. Then he shook his head and bent once more to brush her mouth with his lips. 'For three days only, *mia cara*, and then we will—make up, *no*?'

It was all happening so fast, Sara thought dazedly, and clung to that warm sensual mouth for as long as she was able. The familiar combination of masculine scents teased her senses, and the warmth of his body leaned towards her were sensations she relinquished very reluctantly.

'The moment I am home, Sara *mia*, I will call you and we will go somewhere and eat and talk, somewhere quiet. Perhaps to Bennot's, where you can have the peaches and *granita*, *si*?'

'*Si*!'

She laughed at her own attempt to copy his Italian, and Carlo reached across the counter for her, pulling her towards him, and impatient at the barrier between them. He smiled down into her flushed and smiling face and traced the outline of her mouth with one long forefinger, pressing down her lower lip before letting her go.

'Three days only, *bella mia*, and I will come for you!'

For the first time she noticed the briefcase he had deposited on the counter, and it somehow gave her a sense of reassurance. He was going away for three days, but the signs were that he was going somewhere on business, and he had promised to come for her as soon as he came back. There was nothing more she could hope for.

'I'll still be here!'

Her laughter was unsteady and he once more leaned across and kissed her, leaving his lingering warmth on her mouth. '*Certamente* you will be here, *carissima mia* —if you are not be sure I will find you!'

Sara's heart was drumming wildly and her eyes when they looked up at him were wide and bright and incapable of hiding what she felt. 'Carlo, if you——'

'I am so late, *piccola*, I cannot stay longer, much as I long to!' His hand smoothed softly over her flushed cheek and he smiled. *'Ciao, bella mia!'* Another brief kiss and he was gone, with barely time for her to call after him.

'Ciao, Carlo!'

It seemed no more than a few seconds since he had come in through the door, and already he was on his way out again, and she realised how much her whole outlook had changed in that short time. Turning in the doorway, he gave her a brief salute that was part wave, then strode off across the square towards the nearest waterway, probably to where he had the motor launch waiting.

She could watch him from the window until he disappeared into the narrow dimness of one of the *calles*, and she was unaware at first that she had her hands pressed so tightly to her breast over the thudding beat of her heart. It was different, she told herself over and over again. It *was* different; he would come back to her as he had promised.

Sara was too immersed in her own involvement with Carlo to give much thought to anyone else's affairs, but she nevertheless let Cris know how things stood with Gianni and Maria. She wasn't sure just what she expected his reaction to be, but it was clear that he was far from being the brokenhearted lover his impassioned declaration of undying love had led her to expect.

He talked about Maria quite easily and willingly and

showed a definite interest in the fact that so far there was unlikely to be any change in the plans for her to marry Gianni when she was a little older. It must be marvellous, Sara thought, to recover so completely from what had seemed to be an undying love, and she mused, not without envy, on her own case. Carlo had promised that he would come back to her and she believed he meant it, but still somewhere in the back of her mind was a niggling doubt that it could be in any way permanent.

As usual Signor Vincenti was not at home, but Cris was, and he sat out on the balcony garden with Sara and his mother, stretched out on a chair with his eyes closed and a look of such contentment on his good-looking young face it was almost smug. At other times Signora Vincenti would have chided him to go out and see his friends, but since his unexpected flight from the bosom of his family, she was doing everything possible to keep him beside her for fear he repeated the episode.

'Aren't you going out tonight, Cris?'

Sara looked across at him and smiled, catching his eye as she did so and noting the bright gleam of laughter in their depths. 'Not tonight, Sara—are you not going out somewhere?'

He was teasing her, she knew it, but it was something she was growing used to and found less embarrassing as time went on. Instead she looked pointedly at the English magazine she was reading and made believe she did not hear Signora Vincenti's soft cluck of reproach for her son.

'No, Cris, not tonight.'

She should have known, of course, that Cris would not be content to leave it there, and his dark eyes sought hers, insisting that she look at him, and when she did he smiled broadly. 'Ah, but Signor Carlo Cantorini is out of town, *si*?'

'Crispino!'

Sara had been expecting something of the sort, but even so she felt the warmth of colour in her cheeks that gave away the accuracy of his guess, and Signora Vincenti was appalled by his boldness. She would have scolded him more thoroughly, Sara guessed, but she shook her head slowly and his mother subsided.

'Carlo's away for a few days on business—but I'll be seeing him when he comes back tomorrow.'

Obviously it was still a matter of concern to Signora Vincenti, that she was still seeing Carlo, and she was looking at her doubtfully. 'You will be seeing *il signore* again, Sara?'

'Most certainly I will!' She thought her quite mad, Sara knew, but she was in no mood to be deterred, not when Carlo would be coming back tomorrow. She found the waiting almost unbearable at times. 'I saw Signor— Carlo just before he left on this trip; he came to the shop to see me.'

'He came while I was not there.' Cris added the information hastily, and made sure his mother did not miss the significance of it by nodding and pursing his lips.

It was clear that Signora Vincenti was not at all happy about it, though she probably realised there was little she could do, and once more Sara pondered on the character of her hostess. She had become quite fond of Cris's mother while she had been under her roof, but she saw no hope of ever getting her to see that she was capable of taking care of herself.

Signora Vincenti had had a large family and she was

the eternal mother figure. She worried as a matter of course about anyone and everyone who came within her sphere, whether they were her family or not. Her interest was kindly meant, Sara knew, but she wished the older woman could take a less prejudiced view of Carlo.

'I don't know why you should find it so significant that Carlo came to the shop while you weren't there, Cris,' she told him, a hint of impatience in her voice that Cris did not fail to notice. 'You were out rather a lot that day. You didn't see Gianni when he came either—to tell me that you'd been to the villa to see him.'

It was a subject she had so far said very little about, and she saw the swift sideways glance he gave his mother when Sara mentioned his visit to the Villa Cantorini. Signora Vincenti obviously knew nothing at all about it, and she said something to her son in their own tongue, her dark eyes bright and angry.

Hastily reverting to English, she looked across at Sara and apologised. 'I am sorry, Sara, if this *bambino* has embarrassed you in any way. *Madre di Dio*, but he is more concern to me than all my other *bambini*! I sometimes despair that I will ever make a good man of him!' She added something more in Italian to the effect that he was too much like his father, but Sara could not understand most of it, and she did not think the Signora intended she should. 'You will forgive him, Sara, *per favore*?'

'Oh yes, of course, I've already forgiven him,' Sara assured her with a smile. 'I suppose it could be said that if he hadn't gone to the villa and told them how—how unhappy I was because I'd quarrelled with Carlo, that Carlo might not have come to the shop to see me before he left. He was in a tremendous hurry and he left almost at once, but he *did* come.' She looked at Cris and pulled a face. 'I suppose I owe him that much.'

'*Grazie, signorina!*'

Cris grinned at her impudently, but she frowned at him, knowing how much his mother disliked his interference on her behalf. 'That's not to say I liked you going and seeing any of the Cantorini family, when I'd specifically asked you not to,' she told him firmly. 'I can handle my own affairs, Cris, without any help from you!'

'So?' He disliked being reprimanded, that was clear, and his dark eyes gleamed across at her, a hint of challenge in his smile. 'Do you also dislike that Signor Giovanni Cantorini plays the matchmaker, Sara?'

Sara's face flamed with colour and she gave Cris a long reproachful look before getting up from her seat and going across to the balcony rail, looking out across the water. The evening shadow show of spires and domes was drawn with dark strokes against the gold-flushed sky, and it was much less disturbing to look at than Cris's bright and all too knowing eyes.

'I don't need you or Signor Cantorini, or anyone else, to play matchmaker, Cris!'

It was clear that an attempt at matchmaking from Carlo's family was news to Signora Vincenti, and it stunned her. Sara could sense her eyes on her even without turning to look at her, and a question was not altogether unexpected, even though she had scolded her son for his intervention.

'*Il vecchiardo* has made an approach to you, Sara?'

She sounded as if she scarcely believed it, and Sara's pulse was suddenly much faster as she clung to the rail of the balcony, her eyes on the lights of Venice where they seemed to float above the reflections of their own brightness. Perhaps she should have taken old Giovanni's interest in her and her grandson more seriously, but she still could not believe that he had expected any more than a passing affair to develop from their association.

'Signor Cantorini invited me out to lunch one day and Carlo happened to be there as well. I'd hardly call it an approach, *signora*.' She spoke without turning round, and her voice sounded vaguely indistinct on the warm evening air as she tried not to give the incident too much importance. 'I liked the old gentleman, he's a bit old-fashioned, but he's very gallant and charming.'

'And very much a—recluse?—so I have heard.'

Signora Vincenti sounded so firmly confident that it was impossible to doubt her, and Sara turned at last and looked at her curiously. The Signora's dark expressive eyes were serious and also curious as she studied her for a second before going on. While Cris watched and listened with undisguised interest.

'It is well known in Venice, Sara, that Signor Giovanni Cantorini does not leave the villa very often since the death of his son many years ago.'

'Carlo's father?'

She had never before questioned the missing generation at the Cantorini villa, now she was avidly interested in knowing all she could regarding Carlo. Signora Vincenti apparently knew more than she had revealed in past conversations, contenting herself until now with issuing warnings regarding Carlo and his son as undesirable company for her.

'There was much pity for him, Sara, for he too had only the one son and it was a tragedy from which he did not easily recover.'

The Cantorini family history seemed to be littered with such tragedies, Sara thought, remembering Gianni's tragically young mother, Carlo's wife. But what concerned her most at the moment was the fact that Giovanni Cantorini was considered to be a recluse who seldom left his home, and yet he had come to the shop and invited her to have lunch with him.

'It—it seems strange that he should bother to come and ask me to lunch, in that case,' she mused, and once more felt both pairs of dark eyes watching her in the evening light.

'Very strange, Sara!'

That was Cris, of course, but she was too preoccupied for the moment to pay him attention. Old Giovanni had obviously known his grandson would be lunching at that restaurant, and his tactics had become even more obvious when he left them after only one course, to finish the rest of the meal alone together. Carlo, she recalled, had been less embarrassed by it than she had herself.

She turned and looked at the Signora when her soft but insistent voice broke once more across her thoughts. 'It seems *il vecchiardo* has a high regard for you, Sara!'

The implication was unmistakable, but even Carlo had claimed that his grandfather had a soft spot for her, and it seemed that Signora Vincenti shared his view. With his reputation as a recluse in mind, if he had indeed ventured out with the specific intention of inviting her to lunch and of bringing her and Carlo together, then perhaps she should have taken his matchmaking as seriously as Carlo had, although it was hard to believe it, even now.

'Do you not agree that Signor Giovanni Cantorini seems to have a high opinion of you, Sara?'

Cris's voice, quiet but threaded with the laughter so that she knew he was smiling, invited her to comment, but she was unwilling to be drawn too far. Things were suddenly going rather too fast for her, and she kept her head turned from him as she answered, looking instead at the lights that danced on the water and the dreamlike shapes silhouetted against the darkening sky.

'It seems possible,' she said.

CHAPTER TEN

It was scarcely credible that four days had gone by since Carlo's hurried call at the shop to tell her he would be away for three days, for time had never gone so slowly before. Sara hardly expected to have first consideration when he came back, so she had not expected him yesterday, but today he would certainly be coming and she could do nothing about the almost sickening sense of excitement she felt.

She was working over near the door, where she could see clear across the square, and several metres in either direction as well, so she was bound to see him coming. It was a device that Cris had seen through easily enough, but she was in no mood to care whether or not he found her preoccupation amusing.

While she busied herself setting out some charming little St Cloud porcelain figures, her mind was far away, but she was suddenly aware of Cris standing at her elbow, and she looked up at him and smiled inquiringly. Even then he had only half her attention, for she managed at the same time to glance out into the sunlit square once more.

Cris's gaze switched rather pointedly in the direction of the clock on the wall behind the counter, and he pulled a face. 'Are we not to have lunch today, Sara?'

'Oh, good heavens!' She looked at her wristwatch and laughed. 'I'm sorry, Cris. Look, you go on without me, will you? I won't bother about anything today, I'll just— wander around somewhere. In case Carlo comes,' she added with a hint of defiance for the sudden flick of black brows and the bright mischievous eyes that teased her unmercifully.

'You will not have lunch?'

The idea of going without food was beyond Cris's comprehension, and she laughed at him, pushing him out of the door as she did so. 'I don't need lunch, and the exercise will do me good!'

'Ah, you will live on love, *si*?' He rolled his eyes and used his hands with such expressive meaning that she felt herself blushing like a schoolgirl. 'The breaker of hearts, eh Sara? You have captured him, I think!'

'I wouldn't know!'

She shook her head at him as he went out into the sunny square, then went across and picked up her handbag, mulling over what Cris had said. It was doubtful if anyone would ever capture Carlo Cantorini for very long, but at the moment she was too involved to think beyond the present and the fact that he had promised to come and see her when he came back. It was all she wanted to think about.

By the time she had locked the shop door Cris was nowhere to be seen, and she wandered rather aimlessly across the square with nothing definite in mind, but heading instinctively in the direction of the nearest waterway. Across the square and down the narrow *calle* opposite, to where a small hump-backed bridge spanned the canal. If Carlo was coming during her lunch hour he was almost bound to come by boat, and she would be there to meet him.

The canal was busy as always, just as city streets are busy in the rush hour, and the little hump-backed bridge was surging with people, back and forth like a garrulous tide of warm humanity. It wasn't easy, but she found herself a place on the bridge where she could stand and look down at the water, with eyes that were vaguely distant as she watched the *vaporetti* plying back and forth, and the *motoscàfi* scuttling like beetles among the slower craft.

The sky was a golden blue, hazed with the heat of the day, and shimmering above the rooftops like shot silk. She had been familiar with such scenes ever since she was a child, through the works of the old masters, but only in Venice could an artist's interpretation become a reality. The same breathtaking beauty given depth by the mobility of life.

After a time the variety of craft going back and forth below the bridge ceased to have any individuality and became simply part of a scene; but then one came into her line of vision suddenly that struck a note of familiarity, and she raised her head quickly when she recognised the Cantorini motor launch.

The sunlight on the screen in front of the man at the wheel turned it dazzlingly opaque, but the man himself was tall enough for his head to show above it, and her heart gave a sudden frantic leap when she recognised the dark arrogant head and strong brown face. Dark glasses shaded his eyes from the dazzle of the sun, and the light wind stirred his hair into untidiness as he tipped back his head.

Forgetting her usual inhibitions, Sara raised herself on to her toes and raised her hand to wave, but at that moment she saw something that had been hidden from her until now. As the launch came nearer the bridge, the sun no longer glared across the glass screen and she could see through it into the well of the boat.

Standing beside Carlo, with one hand tucked familiarly through his arm as he guided the craft through the traffic, was the dark woman she had first seen at the restaurant where Carlo took her to dinner. She felt dazed for a moment, as if she had been slapped very hard, and the hand she had half raised to wave fell limply to her side.

He mustn't see her. That was the thought uppermost in her mind as she turned away, walking on legs that felt scarcely able to carry her. He mustn't know that she had been watching for him, for he would not easily forgive her for embarrassing him when he was with another woman. As she turned, she caught a glimpse of a hand raised in greeting; at least she thought she did, but her eyes were already filling with tears, and there was a coldness in her heart that made her feel suddenly very small and lonely.

He could not know how she felt, she thought, he would not have behaved as he had otherwise, for she refused, even now, to believe he was intentionally a cruel man. While she had been awaiting his return with such naïve excitement he was already back and seeing one of his old flames. She fumbled with the key in the lock and made her way blindly across the shop to the room at the back. It shouldn't surprise her, and it shouldn't hurt so much, for she knew his reputation. A breaker of hearts, Signora Vincenti had called him, and she had thought her own heart in no danger—now she had been made to see how wrong she was.

Thankful that there were very few clients during the afternoon, Sara said little, and even the ebullient Cris had been quiet and subdued, though she had said nothing to him about seeing Carlo. It was almost as if he knew everything had gone wrong, and he was hesitant about telling her the identity of the caller when the telephone rang shortly after he arrived back.

'Signor Carlo Cantorini?' He turned and looked at Sara and she shook her head anxiously, her eyes blinking back the tears that threatened, but determined to be firm this time.

'I regret, *signore*, that Signorina Ramson is not yet returned from her lunch.' He listened for a second, then nodded and replaced the receiver. '*Si, signore.*'

Obviously curious, Cris looked at her as he came across, his dark eyes not only curious but anxious too, and she thought he suddenly seemed more grown-up. He leaned on the counter beside her, his hands clasped together and not looking at her while he spoke, as if he feared she might not welcome his intervention.

'Sara, I hope that this—I hope that I have not done anything to cause this sorrow for you.'

Impulsively she reached out and took his hands, trying to smile, though it did not reach her eyes. 'Of course not, Cris. It has nothing to do with anything you've done, it's just that I've been—stupid, that's all.' She laughed very unsteadily and shook her head, trying to get rid of the tears that threatened. 'I was warned, by both you and your mother.'

'The breaker of hearts,' Cris repeated softly, and shook his head. 'But you were so looking forward to his return this morning, Sara. I do not understand.'

He meant well and he was sympathetic, but he was too young to look upon as a confidante, and Sara shook her head at the invitation to confide. 'There's nothing to understand, Cris. Just—forget about it, that's all.'

He said nothing more, but his dark eyes constantly turned in her direction and she thought he was unhappy because she was. If only she could have been more reassuring, but she felt much too low herself to think of consoling anyone else. It was less than half an hour later when the telephone again summoned Cris to answer it, and, as before, he looked at Sara inquiringly when the caller spoke.

It took all the will-power she possessed, but Sara shook her head as she had the last time, and Cris, with obvious reluctance passed on the message that she was not yet returned from lunch. It was clear that by now Carlo would know she had seen him and her heart was thudding hard as Cris replaced the receiver and turned to face her. He would not come, she was sure, he was much too proud to try and placate her when he had been so firmly snubbed, and she felt more numbly cold than ever.

With a small and valuable piece of Nove porcelain in her hands Sara swung round hastily when the door opened suddenly, almost dropping it when she found Carlo's tall, menacing figure standing so close she could feel the heat of passion that consumed him.

His eyes looked so dark they were almost black and they gleamed like jet in the arrogant darkness of his face as he looked down at her for several seconds before he spoke. Then it was to Cris, who stood behind the counter watching with bright, curious eyes.

He said something in Italian, and Cris glanced at Sara. What it was she had no idea, but Carlo repeated himself and added more for good measure, sending Cris scuttling for the shop key which he put without hesitation into

Carlo's hand. Sara's hand was grasped firmly and the key put into it, her stiff fingers curled up to encompass it while dark eyes watched her steadily.

'Lock the door, Sara!'

She was trembling like a leaf, unprepared for such events and yet helpless to do anything to change them. She glanced at Cris, his good-looking young face a mixture of pleasure and avid curiosity, and she shook her head vaguely as she looked at the key in her hand.

'I can't——' she began, and the hand holding her wrist became steel-hard, the long fingers refusing to let her break free of them.

'Send the boy away and lock up, Sara, I cannot speak to you while there is a chance of being interrupted. *Vieni!* Do as I say, Sara!'

She looked at Cris, helpless to defy the authority of that deep, strong voice, and Cris was already standing with his hand on the door. 'You'd—I think you'd better go, Cris. I don't know——'

'*Si, si!*' He seemed willing enough to oblige and he ducked out of the door and into the sunshine while she still stood with the key in her hand. '*Ciao, bella* Sara!'

He hurried past the window, raising a hand in salute, and as he went out of sight Carlo took the key from her and locked the door, making sure it was secure before he turned and took her arm. Unresisting, she went with him, through the opening in the counter and into the back room behind the drawn curtain where it was cool and shadowed and lit only by a small window high up in one wall.

Carlo looked around him, his mobile mouth making a brief grimace of wry humour at the sparseness of their surroundings. Then he put his hands on Sara's arms and turned her until she stood facing him, his dark eyes looking down at her with that same disconcerting steadiness.

'This is not the place I would choose for such a moment,' he told her, his voice more familiarly soft and quiet so that she felt a shiver course along her back at the sound of it. 'But the choice is yours, *carissima*, you would not speak with me and arrange somewhere more suitable.'

'More—suitable?'

She had not yet looked at him and he raised her face with a finger under her chin, so that she could feel the intensity of the dark eyes trying to read her expression even without seeing them. 'Why did you refuse to speak to me, Sara?'

She wished she was not so headily aware of that sense of urgency about him, and the strong vigour of the hands that held her so that she could not move, even had she wanted to. 'Cris told you——'

'The boy lied because you told him to! Do you think me too much a fool to realise that he would have spoken to me in Italian if you had not been here with him? No, *diletta mia*, I knew that you were here and would not speak to me—now I am here to discover why!' He raised her face, his hand under her chin, and kissed her lips, just lightly so that she felt a sudden urgent fluttering sensation in her breast. 'You will tell me, *si*?'

'Oh, Carlo, you *know* why!' The long darkness of her lashes still hid her eyes from him and he bent his head once more to kiss the closed lids. 'I—I saw you with——' She shrugged uneasily, realising for the first time that she did not even know the dark woman's name. 'I don't know who she is, but I know——'

'You know nothing, *carissima*, but you guess much, and you guess wrongly. Will you let me explain, *no*?'

How could she refuse? Sara thought wildly. She wanted him to be just as he was now, she had dreamed of it ever since he left her four days ago with that promise to come back for her, and she nodded silently.

'You think I have—what is it?—played you false, *no*?'

'Not that!' She denied it hastily, looking up at him at last and finding the dark eyes so glowing and warm that she did not want to lose sight of them again. 'I—I thought you were just seeing another woman, that's all.'

'That is all!' he repeated softly, his hands pulling her to him, until she was close to the taut, muscular strength of him and aware of every vibrant nerve that strained her closer still. 'I told you that I would come and find you, did I not, *carissima mia*? But you could not trust me.'

'I—I wanted to, but I thought with you coming home yesterday, and then——'

'I was delayed for another day, Sara *mia*. If I had returned yesterday I would have been *here* yesterday.' One hand stroked her cheek, the palm warm and soothing on her soft skin. 'Did you not realise that, *cara mia*?'

Sara wanted desperately to believe it and in her heart she already did. Only in her mind's eye she kept seeing that sleek, dark woman beside him, with her arm through his, standing beside him in the launch as if she had every right to be there.

'It was just seeing you with someone else. I—I didn't know what to think.'

'Oh, *piccola mia*!' His arms were around her so tightly that she could not have moved even had she the slightest inclination to, and his face rested on the softness of honey-gold hair that muffled his voice. 'You find it hard to trust me, *si*? I cannot find it in my heart to blame you, *amante*, for I have no one to blame for the man I have been but myself!'

'Who—who is she, Carlo?'

She looked up at him, her grey eyes begging him to let her down lightly. It wasn't easy to question him about the dark woman at such a moment, but she was much too unsure of herself and of Carlo to go blindly on without knowing. Strong fingers caressed her neck with exquisite tenderness and he kissed her brow just where the honey-gold hair began.

'She is—an old acquaintance, *carissima*. I met her by accident and knowing that I was going home, she asked that I should drive her where she wanted to go. Since it was on my way, there was little else I could do for the sake of good manners.' Dark eyes looked down into her face and for a second he smiled ruefully. 'If I had known that you were to be waiting on that bridge for me, *amore mia*, I swear I would not have concerned myself with good manners, I would have driven home alone!'

His eyes had a glowing darkness that sent little shivers of excitement through her, and Sara knew he must see the love she had for him quite clearly in her face as she looked up at him, but there was nothing she could do about it now. He held her more tightly than ever, and the dark, avid gaze that was fixed so hungrily on her mouth made her senses reel.

'Oh, Sara, *carissima mia*, can you not forgive me? Not just for this but for everything I have ever done that could hurt you?' His voice had a vibrant urgency that was irresistible, like the arms that bound her to him, and she knew she would forgive him anything just to be where she was at this moment. 'My love, will you not believe that I am so much in love with you that I cannot rest for the torment of it? I have loved you so much and I have needed so desperately to tell you!'

'Carlo!'

His dark eyes glowed with an intensity that ran through her like fire, and yet she shivered. 'You know what kind of man I have been, Sara; knowing you know has been my torment, for fear you despised me, but now, in your eyes I think—— Will you give me your love, *carissima mia*, as I think you want to?'

'Oh, Carlo, I want to so much, I——'

'Then love me, *diletta mia, per favore*, for I think I shall go mad if you do not!'

Sara no longer felt quite sane. Her emotions were so tangled, so wildly out of control, that she had no strength left to resist. The pressure of his arms around her made her part of the hard vigorous body and stirred passions in her that she had never dreamed of until now. With a light gentle finger she touched his lips.

'Carlo——'

'I love you, *carissima*! I need you and I want you! Oh, God, how I have wanted you!'

His mouth had the hard fierce urgency of desperation, and she was swept along on a tide there was no turning back. Every fibre of her being longed to belong to him, and being in his arms was all she ever wanted—was all she would ever want.

'*Ti amo, carissima mia*—will you marry me?'

Leaning back in the pressing urgency of his arms, Sara looked into the strong, dark face with its glowing eyes and firm wide mouth, then she gave a soft little moan of contentment and rested her forehead against him while she put her arms around his neck and hugged close to him once more.

'I love you,' she whispered in a barely audible voice. 'I want to marry you more than anything in the world, my darling.'

With her head resting on his chest, Carlo stroked her hair, trying it seemed for a second or two to find reasons why she should not become his wife; but now that she was more confident, Sara knew what lay behind it and she smiled as she listened to him.

'We will be living at the Villa Cantorini, *amore mia*, and it is big and not always as comfortable as you might suppose; but it is the home of the Cantorini. Also Nonno, and Gianni too until he marries Maria, will be living with us. Could you accept those conditions, *carissima mia*? Will you still marry me?'

Sara looked up at him, her grey eyes deep and shining and her smile leaving him in no doubt. 'You'll be there with me, Carlo *carissimo mio*,' she said softly, 'and that's all I need.' She looked at him from the shadow of long lashes and her voice was soft and gentle with just a hint of challenge. 'That is if you still want *me*.'

One long finger stroked her neck with sensual gentleness, and he bent his head once more, brushing his lips against the softness of her throat. 'I want you,' he murmured, and sought her mouth again.

Did you miss any of these exciting Harlequin Omnibus 3-in-1 volumes?

Anne Hampson

Anne Hampson #3
Heaven Is High (#1570)
Gold Is the Sunrise (#1595)
There Came a Tyrant (#1622)

Essie Summers

Essie Summers #6
The House on Gregor's Brae (#1535)
South Island Stowaway (#1564)
A Touch of Magic (#1702)

Margaret Way

Margaret Way #2
Summer Magic (#1571)
Ring of Jade (#1603)
Noonfire (#1687)

Margaret Malcolm

Margaret Malcolm #2
Marriage by Agreement (#1635)
The Faithful Rebel (#1664)
Sunshine on the Mountains (#1699)

Eleanor Farnes

Eleanor Farnes #2
A Castle in Spain (#1584)
The Valley of the Eagles (#1639)
A Serpent in Eden (#1662)

Kay Thorpe

Kay Thorpe
Curtain Call (#1504)
Sawdust Season (#1583)
Olive Island (#1661)

18 magnificent Omnibus volumes to choose from:

Betty Neels

Betty Neels #3
Tangled Autumn (#1569)
Wish with the Candles (#1593)
Victory for Victoria (#1625)

Violet Winspear

Violet Winspear #5
Raintree Valley (#1555)
Black Douglas (#1580)
The Pagan Island (#1616)

Anne Hampson

Anne Hampson #4
Isle of the Rainbows (#1646)
The Rebel Bride (#1672)
The Plantation Boss (#1678)

Margery Hilton

Margery Hilton
The Whispering Grove (#1501)
Dear Conquistador (#1610)
Frail Sanctuary (#1670)

Rachel Lindsay

Rachel Lindsay
Love and Lucy Granger (#1614)
Moonlight and Magic (#1648)
A Question of Marriage (#1667)

Jane Arbor

Jane Arbor #2
The Feathered Shaft (#1443)
Wildfire Quest (#1582)
The Flower on the Rock (#1665)

Great value in reading at $2.25 per volume

Joyce Dingwell

Joyce Dingwell #3
Red Ginger Blossom (#1633)
Wife to Sim (#1657)
The Pool of Pink Lilies (#1688)

Hilary Wilde

Hilary Wilde
The Golden Maze (#1624)
The Fire of Life (#1642)
The Impossible Dream (#1685)

Flora Kidd

Flora Kidd
If Love Be Love (#1640)
The Cave of the White Rose (#1663)
The Taming of Lisa (#1684)

Lucy Gillen

Lucy Gillen #2
Sweet Kate (#1649)
A Time Remembered (#1669)
Dangerous Stranger (#1683)

Gloria Bevan

Gloria Bevan
Beyond the Ranges (#1459)
Vineyard in a Valley (#1608)
The Frost and the Fire (#1682)

Jane Donnelly

Jane Donnelly
The Mill in the Meadow (#1592)
A Stranger Came (#1660)
The Long Shadow (#1681)

Complete and mail this coupon today!